# SUPERCENTER

First Montag Press E-Book and Paperback Original Edition May 2013

Montag Press 978-0-9822809-6-6
Cover art © 2013 Jeremy Rathbone
Cover design © 2013 Sam Cowan
Author photo © 2013 Jason Rizos

Montag Press Team:
Project Editor – Jessica Taylor
Layout & E-Book Designer – Sam Cowan
Managing Director – Charlie Franco

A Montag Press Book
www.montagpress.com
Montag Press
536 E. 8th Street
Davis CA, 95616 USA

Montag Press, the burning book with the hatchet cover, the skewed word mark and the portrayal of the long-suffering fireman mascot are trademarks of Montag Press.

Printed & Digitally Originated in the United States of America
10 9 8 7 6 5 4 3 2 1

# SUPERCENTER

## JASON RIZOS

MONTAG

# ACKNOWLEDGEMENTS

This book is dedicated to my wife Krissy, and all my teachers and colleagues, including Catherine Rankovic, Howard Schwartz, Mary Troy, Steve Schreiner, Dave Jenkins, and Trudy Lewis.

I would also like to acknowledge and ask that you read, listen-to, and support the following artistic individuals whose own creative output has helped inspire and form the themes and content of this novel: author and raconteur James Howard Kunstler; author and pop-critic Douglas Rushkoff; author and journalist Chris Hedges; author and sick puppy Mykle Hanson; columnist and political scientist David Michael Green; Marxist Mastermind Brendan Cooney; author and cartoonist David Malki!; off-beat risk-taking author Jason Wuchenich; *Residential Aliens* publisher and editor Lyn Perry; Toronto 8-bit DJ who inspired the soundtrack of the Schwags Touchboy; ambient music artist David "Aperire" Lichtenauer; Portland rock duo *Talkdemonic*; Kmo of the *C-Realm* podcast; Doug Lain of the *Diet Soap* podcast; Lorenzo Hagerty of the *Psychedelic Salon* podcast; The Dopefiend of *The Dopecast* podcast; Jeffrey Rowland's *Overcompensating* and *Wigu* comics; Tim Kreider's *The Pain* comics and associated author statements; Scott Meyer's *Basic Instructions* comics; Brian Sendelbach's *Smell of Steve* comics; and Cenk Uygur of *Wolf PAC* and *The Young Turks* newscast.

The following close friends I'm indebted to for providing insights, encouragement, and first-reads: techno-mage Eric Reinsmidt; writer and cynic Dylan Smith; misanthrope-in-arms Mitch Wells; remarkably grounded life-saver Eric Hernlund; acerbic author and publisher Collin Dodds; academic and writerly consorts Colleen McKee and Jaime Wood; literary champions Kristin Sulis; Gwen Kramer; Jeff and Sharon Handy; bon vivant Mark Cecil; inspiring writer and teacher Ceiridwen Terrill; music aficionado and consummate Missourian Dan Martin; and my never-not-creative father Gus.

And last I would like to thank Jessica Taylor of Montag Press whose keen eye, careful editing, tireless drafting, and inspiring words made *Supercenter* the novel it is today.

*Jason Rizos*

# CHAPTER 1

➲ **Automotive**

**G.E. knew he had not** seen the Supercenter for all that it was. A fresh perspective, he reasoned, would come from atop the shelves. He understood well the tile floor that spanned below. So he climbed the wire-and-pegboard shelving up toward the less understood corrugated steel roof. And above that? Well, Supercenterintendent Benson had told him not to question what lay above, beyond, beneath. It's all consuming, he said. G.E. measured the adult's words carefully. We are all Associates here, Benson said.

Driven by boredom, curiosity, or perhaps simply wishing to gain a new angle, G.E. spontaneously and without forethought decided he must climb the shelves. Upon reaching the top, he walked the balance-beam of iron scaffolding, appreciating the lofty air above, occupied only by the rectangular matrix of black security orbs, pivoting cameras hidden behind one-way glass. The orbs saw all.

The yellow t-shirt beneath his vest asked in bold letters, "How May I Help You?" Framing this, his blue associate vest was decorated with thick black stars of different shapes and sizes, a contribution of his little sister's favorite magic marker. A series of tiny brass safety pins lined the breast on either side of his vest, pins he idly collected from the dressing room

floors and often used to clean snack-food gunk from the trigger and buttons of the infrared Light Rifle slung loosely over
his shoulder. This rifle was an actual US Army issue M4A2,
cast with the same heavy polymer stock, fitted with the same
steel barrel and breech, the chamber replaced with a precision
infrared laser. Per Siege Arena combatant orders, the weapon
never left his side. At least this one rule G.E. obeyed. His curly
shock of uncombed hair, on the other hand, exceeded the
allowed length for a Siege Arena Recruit. Cutting it would
soon become yet another thing Management would tell him
to do. G.E. liked when his hair grew long and set him apart
from the other crew-cut recruits. Any day now, he expected
Benson to at last say something about regulations. G.E. would
then grumble and delay, run his vacuum-trimmer along the
sides of his head only and attempt getting away with a frizzy
mohawk for a day or two until Benson would be forced to say
something yet again.

He would not have long to appreciate his elevated vantage before security would intervene. First, with a call to the
closed-band radio on his belt, and, if he didn't respond, an
overhead page would issue for all to hear. But security, wishing to deprive him the opportunity to flaunt the Supercenter's
rules and regulations before the entirety of the associates—
who would no doubt gawk and cheer him along—did not
make the call.

At the opposite end of the Supercenter, his teacher,
Supercenterintendent Edward Benson, lifted the radio from
his belt and listened to a scratchy, high-pitched voice.

"He's climbing the shelves now," the voice said plainly.

Benson narrowed his eyes. In the distance, he could make

out a figure shambling over Aisle 17. Without hesitation, he presumed this was none other than his most mischievous associate.

"I'll take care of it." He spoke into his radio and grinned apologetically to the primary school children seated before him. Benson had studied G.E. closely and attributed his self-stylized vest as proof that punk fashion could spontaneously emerge, given the proper availability of metal pins and magic markers. In his choice to mutilate his uniform, a violation of Buy-All policy, G.E. was very much alone among the associates of Supercenter #1501. It infuriated his teacher to no end that G.E. did this because knew he could get away with it—Management would not soon reprimand their star performer. The sooner that changed the better, Benson surmised.

G.E. stepped gently along the shelf beams, hands stretched out to either side. Beneath him, stretched rows of parallel aisles, shelves of steel and wire, a plastic orchard blooming with blister-packaged fruit. Oblivious to his stunt, off-duty associates harvested a cornucopia of merchandise, neatly sealed in convenient plastic shells and colorful cardboard boxes. The oldest, teenagers like G.E., who had just recently turned thirteen, the rest younger. Some, like his sister, as young as seven. They plucked articles of clothing from silver racks, ordered by color, size, and gender, held hangered articles to their chests briefly, turned tags over in their hands before gently tossing them into their carts. They shopped.

Above, the high-tensile, corrugated steel ceiling of the Supercenter was just a bit closer than ever before. From here, without anything to impede its path, he could sling a plastic CD far and wide—not to mention high—and surely break the distance record. Not that the other Siege Recruits really cared how far he could throw a CD. They humored him with petty distractions like disc slinging, meaningless hijinks compared to gaming on the Siege Arena itself.

As he contemplated this, G.E. rested his hand upon a hollow pillar of shelf scaffolding, where he felt a sliver of thick paper protrude. He couldn't imagine what could be crammed here, or for what reason, what had to have been ages ago. G.E. picked at it until he at last slid a massive paper roll from the pillar. A decade of dust and cobweb drifted softly to the tile below. G.E. wasted no time. He turned, knelt, braced himself against the shelving, and eagerly unfurled the heavy paper upon a box containing 144 individually packaged ramen soups.

He unfurled a bizarre artifact—light-blue ink printed on soft, indigo vellum. It did not take him long to recognize this as a map of the Supercenter itself. A terrifically detailed, schematic blueprint of the Supercenter. Unfamiliar terms ran at perpendicular angles along the map—"Acoustic Noise Filter," "Variable Air Volume," "Wall Return Joist" along with numerals and acronyms G.E. did not understand, most prominently, the title. The entire diagram was labeled at the top with thin capital letters:

#### #1501 - H V A C   S C H E M A T I C

The most startling detail on this document, however, was its margins. The Supercenter, it seemed, did indeed have an exit. G.E. had, as had the other children raised within the Supercenter's four walls, simply presumed it was one among perhaps an infinite number of others, tucked together like cells in a beehive. Like a bubble bursting beneath the sea, his subconscious reeled from this sudden and jarring spatial expansion of his rectangular universe. The only discreet thought that entered his mind as he studied the blueprint was a seeping resignation that he should—that he inevitably must—investigate the spaces that lie beyond the Supercenter's interior.

"Mr. Westinghouse," Supercenterintendent Benson's voice boomed below him. Benson's face was ruddy and pock-marked—years of artificial light had not been kind to his complexion. He wore his black hair in an unflinching, perfect part, with an immaculately trimmed mustache to match.

G.E. frantically rolled up the blueprint, but it was no use. "What is that?" Benson asked. "What have you got there?"

"Uh…." G.E. hurried for an answer. "I'm not sure, really."

"Hand that over, this instant!" Benson snapped his fingers and pointed an open palm to G.E., a good twenty feet above. G.E. cursed himself for opening it outside of his home compartment, which occupied the shelf directly below. He shimmied down to the floor and presented the document.

"This…." Now it was Benson's turn to come up with answers. "Is nothing." G.E. noticed his eyes dart to the left, looking at nothing in particular.

"It looks like some kind of instructions for building a Supercenter," G.E. said, disbelieving his own words. The very notion of a Supercenter being *built* was outrageous. Built out of what? Built on what? Where? And what could have possibly existed before it? Benson began hurriedly rolling up the blueprint.

"This is just some preposterous artwork," Benson said, but to G.E. this in no way resembled his sister's finger-painted portraits. This drawing was angular, measured, exact.

"But what about this area?" G.E. pointed as the blueprint curled beneath Benson's fingers. "With all these hash marks. 'Outlot' it says. What does that mean?"

"Enough. I'm confiscating this. I can already see it's leading to trouble."

"What?" G.E. contested.

"Exactly what were you doing up on top of your shelf?" Benson shot back at him.

"Nothing. Just looking around, I guess."

"It is always *nothing* with you. Remapping buttons on the other recruits' Light Rifles. Downloading contraband software on the Buy-Net. Leaving skid marks along the floor with that insipid skateboard that you insist on riding everywhere you go. Tell me, G.E., do you appreciate what a privilege it is to compete on the Siege Arena whatsoever? Do you know there are several associates here who will never have the opportunities for gaming that you enjoy each day?"

"Yessir...." G.E. said meekly. He did feel guilty, nearly all the time, that he had qualified for Siege Arena duty and had only to practice video games as his job, rather than maintain the merchandise or clean the Supercenter, like so many of the other associates.

"Very well then. You won't speak of this again, do you understand?"

G.E. said nothing, his mind already turning toward exploration.

"You know, The G.M. has taken a shine to you," Benson

said. "Frankly, I don't know what he sees in you, but he has hesitated to revoke your play time as a disciplinary action. Do not expect this to continue." He turned away to punctuate the severity of this statement, but not without adding, "And do something about that hippie mop of yours."

As the Supercenterintendent walked away with the blueprint, G.E. drew his bangs out with his fingers and looked up to appreciate their length. He lifted his board from where it rested against the shelf support, tossed it to the floor, and stepped aboard. He thought only of one adult who could provide answers. But first, he would need something to offer in return.

Leg pumping, G.E. skated away from Office Supplies. Clack, clack, clack. The floor, slick and waxen, sped beneath translucent rubber wheels. He dodged through a sparse crowd of slow-moving associates. In their reverie, the shoppers experienced depressed metabolisms and lowered heart rates, their brains flooded with *norepinephrine,* their pupils dilated. An associate reached for a pack of adhesive rhinestones as G.E. slipped between him and the shelf, ducking under an outstretched arm. In the serene state of retail abandon, G.E.'s swift path, sharp turns, near collisions, and reckless speed did not disturb them in the slightest.

He stopped briefly by the Electronics Department. Unseen by the other associates, he reached beneath a locked glass counter and slipped a small box into his messenger bag. He then turned down the far most aisle and pointed himself toward the outskirts—Automotive.

Nobody traveled the outskirts of the Supercenter any longer, not since the United Associates Cooperative took over and began occupying these increasingly sparse and broken-down shelves. Here, as the shelves turn bare, they at last devolve into a solitary, blockaded aisle—39—into which no respectable associate ventured. Aisle 39, a last-ditch salvation for associates unwilling or perhaps unable to participate in the great consumer enterprise that was Buy-All Supercenter #1501. They were the unassociates. And, as G.E. neared their epicenter, he spotted them, floaters and lowlifes, dozing on busted plastic furniture, shanghaied on its way to the trash chute. Supercenterintendent Benson forbade not just G.E. and the other Siege Arena recruits, but all associates from ever setting foot among the abandoned aisles, let alone Aisle 39. Benson hated the UAC, called them the Demise of Civilization.

The crowd of shoppers thinned as G.E. made his way to the outer perimeter. The merchandise evaporated until only barren pegboard and slanted diagonals of half-collapsed shelves remained. Hearing the clack of his skateboard on the tiles, a few squatter unassociates poked their heads from behind bedsheet-curtained shelves and regarded him lazily. G.E. did not resent the unassociates mingling around Aisle 39. He felt sorry for them, those with nothing to live for and nowhere to go. As his thoughts turned despondent, he reminded himself that surely Management would take them back—if they asked. Most likely.

He thought instead of his objective. An adult dwelled within Aisle 39, for years now, without showing himself to anyone. Today, G.E. would chance visiting this legendary hermit. This journey took him where he had never ventured, to the farthest corner, obscured by the tarp-and-blanket covered Aisle 39 and the *de facto* leader of the unassociated. G.E. pressed the tail of his skateboard, unconcerned about the long black smear left on the tile. A blue plastic tarp hung across the threshold. Upon the end caps on either side, row upon row of plaster human skulls—decoration, items not for sale.

Two unassociates stood guard outside the forbidden aisle. Sentry duty, they called it. G.E. heard rumors of what lay inside, but only unassociates themselves were permitted. Beneath oversized, metal-studded leather jackets, they wore Lacrosse shoulder and elbow pads, and on their heads unfastened hockey helmets. Casually, G.E. tried to pass through the blue tarp threshold, but they crossed makeshift halberds before him—a steel curtain rod and a long bamboo tiki torch. One sentry G.E. recognized. He was about his age, and no doubt had paid his dues in the Siege Arena before quitting. Or, more likely, he failed to qualify for graduation and decided then to join up with the UAC.

"Long way from home, soldja-boy." He affected a tough voice and squeezed the curtain rod with both hands.

G.E. involuntarily cast a glance up at the nearest black security orb, hanging from a long metal post on the ceiling. "I'm here to see Brett," he said.

"He's not expecting you."

"I've never been here before."

"We know."

G.E. turned his back to the security orb, a futile gesture, as this only put him in the line of sight of another. He carefully opened his messenger bag, just wide enough to offer the sentry a peek. "I'm sure you don't have one of these?"

The sentry regarded this with a smirk. This visitor would not easily scare, like so many other associates seeking council with the only renegade adult in the entire Supercenter.

"Alright, Gameboy, you just wait here." He lifted a shoulder to the other sentry, who quickly disappeared behind the curtain.

"Besides, ain't you got some Schwags to frag?" he asked, alluding to the enemy monsters hunted in the Siege Arena. But these were just artificial intelligences. Hoary little zombie creatures that would just throw themselves at you in waves. G.E. had graduated from this opponent two years ago.

"Noobs fight Schwags," G.E. said plainly, without making eye contact. He turned and looked back at the vacant aisle that led away from Aisle 39. At first, the silence was unsettling, but now it was almost peaceful. Beyond them, at the farthest end of Aisle 39, lay the Fourth Corner of the store, unknown and unexplored, hidden beneath the motley tarps that covered the rogue aisle. The sentry caught him grinning at the possibility of discovering secrets within.

"Well, then what you supposed to fight?"

"PvP," G.E. said, but the guard had clearly not advanced this far in his own training. "Player versus player. I fight other recruits. In other Supercenters." He was, however, surprised by the incredulous expression that fell over the guard's face.

"Is that what they tell you?" He laughed. "How you supposed to know there are even other Supercenters out there?"

"We have headsets, genius. We talk about Buy-All stuff all the time." G.E. was not in the mood to debate this paranoid conspiracy drivel with a dropout, not now. Not while standing outside Aisle 39, especially in light of his newfound uncertainty as to the location of the other Supercenters, perhaps not just on the other side of the cinderblock wall as he had been told.

"Do they have Aisle 39 in the other Supercenters?" the sentry asked.

"Sure they do." G.E. brushed him off. "And 36, 35, 34...."

"You know what I mean. The Resistance."

G.E. considered pushing his way past when the other sentry finally returned from behind the curtain and waved him in.

He gave one last look to the guard. "Fighting the AI is pretty easy. But light years harder than standing out here and staring at the floor."

The inside of Aisle 39 resembled all that had been lost or discarded by the greater Supercenter in the past ten years since its closure to the outside world. The most striking difference between this aisle and the rest—aside from the fact that no salable product could be found within this dark hovel—was the repurposing of used-up, trashed merchandise for purposes outside its original intention. An unkempt unassociate dozed upon a small mattress made from twine-fastened plastic laundry detergent bottles. A lampshade built of flattened soup cans cast pinpricks of light upon shelves and a sagging tarp-covered ceiling above. The ceiling itself consisted of shabbily nailed squares of plywood. Holes had been cut into plywood, and colored plastic bottles filled with a few ounces of bleach had been fitted in these holes, which refracted the outside fluorescent light and cast a remarkably bright glow into the enclave, providing usable light while obscuring the aisle from the view of security orbs above. The entire area resembled an elaborate, ornate sarcophagus, sealed with motley bolts of fabric, plastic tarps, bed sheets, and cut panels from cardboard boxes.

But at the rear of the aisle, G.E. spotted a remarkable collection of old fashioned games, from another era. Pinball machines, air hockey, a billiards table, dartboards, a curious kind of shuffleboard-bowling hybrid, and a miniature basketball game wreathed in plastic netting. This rear area was far more inviting than the rest, warmly lit with a soft blue hue, the product of radiant blue neon bar signs and an oversized turquoise lava lamp. A row of classic arcade games, Centipede, Tetris, Ms. Pacman, Arkanoid, and GORF, lined the far wall.

There G.E. found an adult standing before a cantankerous pinball machine named *Bride of Pinbot*. He stood before the machine, and light from the playfield glinted off a silver peace symbol, attached to a heavy, hemp-braided necklace around his neck. Flashing numbers ran down the svelte silver android that was the Bride of Pinbot, reclining on the scoreboard. Behind her, a Space Shuttle blasted toward a red-orange planet. Like G.E., the man's black t-shirt was modified. Several dozen close horizontal cuts ran down the front, beneath which a stark-white abdomen glowed. Over this, he wore a black vinyl vest. He had been growing out a goatee for a long while, and had just enough length to bind it with a tiny red rubber band at the tip. His eyes, naturally sunken and rimmed in darkness, lent a perfect counterpoint to his dark complexion and attire. G.E. thought to himself that this had to be no other than the mysterious Brett Flerchinger himself.

Brett ignored his uninvited guest. G.E.'s head spun around in awe and not watching his progress, he knocked his toe into a coffee table, which sent the lava lamp wobbling, but not quite tipping. The room walls spun with waves of blue as the lava lamp rolled. Brett cast a scowl, the momentary interruption enough to allow his last ball to drain between the flippers.

Brett sighed audibly, walked to a nearby tattered, green-and-white lawn chair and let himself fall. Still without regarding G.E., he retrieved a broken half-pair of scissors from the table beside him, the blade hammered, bent, and meticulously sharpened into a workable knife. He picked up a broken pool cue and set down to whittling, with no apparent goal in mind.

"Are you...." G.E. ventured a guess. "Are you Brett?"

"I don't suppose you've come to turn in your Associate ID and join the cause," Brett grumbled as he shaved the cue. "So let's hope you at least have something of value to offer."

G.E. helped himself to a filthy, broken recliner chair opposite him, careful to remain on the edge. He opened his messenger bag, slipped out a large, black box that could have been made of leather, but was, in fact, a specially-made cardboard. On the center, a single, silver Buy-All star told of the contents within.

"MP3's," G.E. said. "All-Pod players. Chock full of gigabyte goodness." He presented the box and, upon opening, revealed a rainbow of six colored metallic cylinders, each no larger than a tube of lip balm, and set in a white satin interior—red, blue, green, purple, yellow, and black. Brett reached for the black one, but G.E. quickly shut the case. Brett knew immediately that G.E. could not afford six All-Pod players, not when associates saved up months of paychecks for one of their own.

"Stealing?" Brett gave a chuckle. "How is such a thing possible? A Siege Recruit, no less. These things were meant for the Supercenter, no?"

"This *is* the Supercenter and you still have to pay for them."

"Is that so?" Brett put down the knife and pool cue, and brushed curled bits of wood from his lap. "You are still bringing supplies to that old priest, I take it? You steal that as well?"

"That comes out of my own account and is none of your business." With his broken leg, Father Trinity had been on disability leave for nearly eight months now, and, without G.E.'s help, would starve. That, or deal with the UAC, a pact worse than starvation in G.E.'s mind.

"Ah. Your Associate Account. How lovely." Brett moved away from him with a restless urgency, his posture, his gait, unlike the others. Brett's impatience, his entire demeanor, spoke of an ancient past, a place beyond the Supercenter. G.E. tried to infer clues about what this place may be, but the task was hopeless. To G.E., Brett was a relic, an echo of an event that not he nor the other adults would speak of, not to G.E., not to the other associates, not to the unassociates. Nobody. Brett dug into his pocket, produced a pair of quarters, and plunked them into another of his many pinball machines. The coin remained lodged halfway down the chute.

"Everyone seems to think," he grunted as he slammed the machine with his hip, "that they owe something to the Supercenter. That they are forever in its debt. Worthless little peasants at the mercy of their divine lord. Do you feel that way, Gameboy?"

G.E. didn't understand these words "debt" and "peasant." But this was not a surprise. He understood, going into this visit, like with the other adults, the Managers, conversation could run aground at any point. A tense moment of indecipherability, an evocation of that Forbidden Place. From what G.E. gleaned from leaked bits of conversation like this, it was a space larger than the Supercenter itself, perhaps several times larger, perhaps hundreds.

"The All-Pods. Do you want them or not?" G.E. asked.

"I am perfectly capable of stealing from the Merchandise Dock, just like you."

"You won't find any All-Pods on the Merch Dock."

"And why is that?"

"Because I have them. All of them. And there won't be any more until these get counted by the cash registers. This batch will count as merchandise-on-hand until somebody buys them. The Merch Machine doesn't remake stolen merchandise. It will stay registered as stocked inventory until it is scanned at the cash registers."

"Remake?" Brett gave up on the pinball machine and returned to his lawn chair where he resumed whittling to occupy his mind and hands.

"You know, build new ones."

"You really think the *shipping trailer* creates these things? Like some sort of magic oven?"

Ten minutes ago, G.E. would have responded in the affirmative, but now having looked at the HVAC schematic, he did question how neatly stacked, shrink wrapped palettes of merchandise magically appeared behind the roll-up Merch Dock door each month. Huck, his neighbor and Merchandise Lead Associate, called it "the flash." He would even call G.E. on his radio to come watch it on occasion. At one point every month, the edges of the roll-up Merch Dock door turned suddenly brilliant, a bright white light casting long, thin slants of light on the concrete floor, and a smell filling the air unlike anything he had ever smelled before. Minutes later, after a loud crunch, the light disappeared and the door unlocked. Huck then rolled up the door to reveal a long row of neatly stacked palettes of merchandise.

Only five adults occupied the Supercenter, five adults that knew of the time before the Closure. Supercenterintendent Benson was one, but he forbade any discussion of the event. Father Trinity was another, but he was so old and confused now you couldn't take anything he said about the world beyond the four walls seriously. That left the three Department Managers, Oliver Lawrence of Home Furnishings, Vernon Dupre of Jewelry, and, finally, the mysterious Brett Flerchinger.

As if he could read G.E.'s expression, he addressed this point. "Just how old were you when they closed the store?"

"Five."

"Five!" Brett repeated with a mix of astonishment and resignation as he shook his head. "Then you should at least know better. These other kids they adopt—"

"I was not adopted!" G.E. suddenly blurted out. "My parents are coming back for me. And for Nestlé."

Brett paused, thought better of speaking, and looked around his disheveled game room for some other distraction. He didn't have the heart to tell G.E. his parents would not be coming back, that *All Sales Were Final* when it came to the Buy-All Youth Sponsorship Program.

"So, you were one of the first. Have you ever thought about why your parents sold—that is, left you behind?"

"It was too dangerous out there for Nestlé." G.E. couldn't remember if his father told him this or if this was something Supercenterintendent Benson planted in his mind.

"Is that right?"

"Yeah, and they'll probably be back any time."

"Just like all the other parents that come back and get their kids."

G.E. blushed. He hadn't considered that nobody had entered or left the Supercenter in all the time he lived here. He just figured their return imminent and gave no further thought to the possibility they may not.

Brett considered him now, cautiously, and suspected him of a larger agenda, of perhaps seeing the Supercenter for what it truly was—what Brett himself took it for—an illusion taken for granted by all the other children, fostered by video games, a farce, a blip upon the radar of history. *One day the walls will come tumbling down*, Brett thought, *and whoever knocks them down won't bother noticing and won't even care what has been taking place.* He looked at G.E.'s modified assault rifle and then to the wooden stick in his own hand. *This sharpened pool cue will be more valuable to them than an overblown toy video game controller*, he thought.

"You remember playing video games when you were a kid?" Brett asked at last.

"Yeah."

"I do too. I remember you playing video games as a kid. The Electronics Department. I was once the manager."

G.E. raised an eyebrow.

"You don't believe me. Fine. But you brought these All-Pods to me for a reason. Took you this long to muster the courage to come visit Aisle 39. Something must have happened. What are you looking for, anyway? New skateboard? Fleet of skateboards?"

G.E. shifted uncomfortably in his chair. He did not trust Brett, so he resisted asking about the Merchandise Dock, about the creation of product. But if it was not created with the flash, then how else could the merchandise appear so quickly and so completely?

"They say you can open the door...." He trailed off, embarrassed for even asking about such a rumor, spread among the other recruits, along with talk of bizarre rituals, human sacrifice and wild parties, taking place in Aisle 39. He swallowed hard. "The Shuttle Bay door."

Brett leaned forward and whispered, "And what, pray tell, would one find beyond the Shuttle Bay door?"

"Fifteen-oh-three. Fifteen-oh-four," G.E. said. "You know, the other Supercenters."

"Buy-Alls?" Brett asked. "They told you more Buy-Alls surround us?"

G.E. blinked, astonished that anything else could be the case.

"The Outlot," he said at last.

"Where did you hear that word?"

"A map, some kind of assembly instructions for a Supercenter."

"Do you have it?" Brett asked.

"No, Mr. Benson took it from me."

Brett buried his head in his hands.

"But," G.E. began. He revealed a digital camera. In the brief moment before climbing down from the shelf, he had quickly taken a picture of the blueprint, anticipating Benson's confiscation. G.E. pulled up a picture on the LCD screen.

"This..." Brett took the camera, manipulated the buttons, and quickly zoomed in to make the best of the blurry image. "This is informative. Yes...there is a basement, I knew it!"

"What's a basement?" G.E. asked. Brett handed him back his camera. He leapt from his chair and paced while tapping his fist on his chin.

"You are smart, kid. You want to trade those MP3 players for a way out of the Supercenter. That takes guts, kid. And I admire that." He caught G.E. looking away, stealing glances at the four pinball machines at the rear of the aisle. "You know what those are?"

G.E. shook his head slowly.

"Here." Brett stepped over to the well-worn *Funhouse* machine. "It might look dirty, but all the lights, switches, bumpers, they all work just fine." He reached into the open coin door and retrieved the pair of quarters, slung them into a glowing red slot. *What strange trinkets*, G.E. thought without attaching them to currency. He saw a peculiar activation switch, nothing more.

"Go on." Brett waved him to the machine.

G.E. replicated Brett's movement, slung the plunger, watched the ball wrap around the headboard. He snapped the flippers simultaneously with the palms of his hands on the buttons, opening wide the gap between them and clearing the way for the ball to drain straight through.

"Alright," Brett said. "Just a first shot. Now this time, think about how hard you want to pull that plunger. And those flippers, try them out. They don't just have an on and off do they? Only press them as hard as it takes to get them to flip." G.E. tried this, the flippers bounced reflexively, gingerly ticked up and down, as if tamed by his gentle force. "Like that. And never hold them open unless you are trapping the ball." Brett went on to explain the trap, holding the ball inside an open flipper, leaning down to aim a left flipper shot into the Hidden Hallway, a right flipper shot into the Mystery Mirror. Once G.E. learned to keep the ball in play, Brett taught him strategy, of saving the high-point shots and multiball until the other bonuses were maxed out. The playfield entranced. Here was a game made of solid objects and physical motion. Unlike the software-dependent games of the Siege Arena, here the possibilities were infinite.

His guest now fully engrossed, Brett sat back and allowed G.E. to repeatedly sling the quarters back into the coin slot and master the playfield. After he got the hang of it, Brett jumped back in. "Okay, then. Now we go head-to-head. Win, and I'll trade you those All-Pods for a key to the Shuttle Bay doors."

"And if I lose?"

"Then you take your trinkets back to TV Land."

G.E. did not object, eager for just another round on the machine. Whether he won outright or if Brett let the count-down on the Superdog expire to lose by just 30,000 points was uncertain. But, with a sporting equanimity, Brett conceded defeat. He produced from his pocket a solitary brass key strung on a pillowy, white shoelace and set it gently into G.E.'s open hand.

"Now, you can't tell anyone that you got this from me, okay?"

"Of course." G.E. handed over the black box.

"You forgot one more thing." Brett lifted the key above his head.

"Benson. Look, I'm not worried about the Supercenterintendent."

"What are you going to tell Benson when he asks about your little visit today?"

"He won't."

"Yeah right he won't."

"I'll tell him to get fragged. Besides, I'll be gone before he knows it."

"Wait for nightfall. You don't want them to see you at the door. This will buy you time on the other side."

G.E. at once threw his skateboard to the floor of the cluttered aisle, rolled over the gritty tile, unswept and unpolished for years.

"Eager little twerp," Brett mumbled as he opened up the box. He turned over the black All-Pod, *this one I'll keep for myself*, he thought. He was surprised to find the screen turned on. He pressed play. Nothing. Track backwards, forwards. The thing was stuck on Shelly Arkansas' *Buy-All Hoochie-Koo,* some insipid pop country pap he would delete as soon as— Brett touched the screen. He ran his fingernail along the edge and it peeled back, a sticker on a hollow shell. He reached for the red, then the blue player.

Demo units, all.

# CHAPTER 2

 Electronics

**The Electronics Department no longer** resembled the sparse, technologically humble Electronics Department of the pre-closure era. Then, precious square footage was squandered for copious digital video disks with their tedious packaging and tiered racks, sample televisions sporting the same identical looping advertisements, myriad overpriced inkjet printer cartridges, and specious desktop publishing software suites. Today's Buy-All Electronics Department squeezed merchandise tighter than a Hong Kong bazaar. Continuous glass display counters were trimmed with colorful neon lights that adorned electrical gadgetry of every shape, size, and flavor. Cameras, closed-band radios, MP3 players, watches, laser pointers, light-up jewelry, digital photo frames, laptop computers, hand-held Siege Arena devices, and, last but not least, Christmas lights—the trendiest way of accessorizing one's home compartment.

Beyond the baroque racks, heavy-gauge yellow and black extension cords spilled from the department in long, radial slants, like the sinewy tentacles of some magnificent cephalopod. Every electrical outlet in the department was fully capacitated. Hence, cables reached out to outlets along Center Aisle in their thirst for electricity.

The greater Supercenter outside the Electronics Department measured over 10,000 square feet. But, for the recruits who competed therein, the inside of the Electronics Department was infinite. The attention of each recruit focused on the centerpiece of the department—a panoptic arc of three 72" plasma screens that combined for an extraordinarily wide peripheral field of vision. The screens, arranged in a curve, assured the recruits that no other place, no other time, mattered more, certainly not the potato chip dusted carpet and tile floor that lurched backwards from the screen.

The din of combat from two dozen Siege Arena consoles, plus the ambient music beaming from high-fidelity speakers, beckoned G.E. to spend the remainder of his day lost in their siren's song. Greeted by metallic synthesizers and the metric beat of trance music, G.E. flicked his skateboard into his hand and stepped over the twisting cables and into the gaming den within. He pushed his way past a dozen or so recruits, some senior recruits like him, others only eleven or twelve years old, on leave from the Education Department.

He scarcely remembered his parents, yet vivid were the memories of the first time he played the Siege Arena. The video games he remembered all too well, every map, arena, dungeon, and citadel. And he remembered being told he was a special case—that other kids his age would be moved to facilities or customer service if they did not test as well with the Siege Arena. And now, after all this time climbing the rankings, G.E. had earned an all-access pass. The library of games spanned a dozen consoles and decades too distant to count. He could invest a lifetime exploring multitudinous digital realms. All that was asked in return was that he maintain his competitive form on the Siege Arena's Tactical Combat Engine. But now, having discovered the Supercenter blueprints, he could think of no other place worthy of his attention but the possibility of a space beyond its four walls.

Another all-access recruit, his friend Trident, sat right up front and center, in his Aerial Combat chair, fitted with flight yoke, floor pedals, and a panel of knobs, switches, and buttons. Trident kept the blond hair on his squareish head nice and short. Unlike the other recruits, he was stocky and muscular despite the fact that nobody got any serious exercise. He looked like the kind of kid who would be too bulky and strong to properly finesse the Siege Arena, but this couldn't be any farther from the truth.

A vast, digitalized landscape stretched out before him. Because the recruits had no clue what the Earth's actual horizon looked like, no effort was placed in replicating it. The Siege Arena landscapes were harsh, geometric, planar, green fields overlaid with a tan grid, offering only enough perspective to get the job done. Trident twisted and pulled his virtual craft around the empty sky, executing evasive maneuvers, as rockets sailed from behind and billowed smoky contrails as they passed him.

Trident pumped the pedals, gently, quietly, with no sense of urgency. His strength held in check, he never mashed the controls, never swung his thick arms around to coax his aircraft into some semblance of stability. Not that G.E. couldn't pilot the digital helicopter. He just couldn't do it well. For starters, he always contended, why not make up go up? Why must up go down and down send the thing up? With enough study, one could manage to lift the thing up and effortlessly fly it in a straight line, a feat in itself. Or one could somehow manage to intuit the controls and pull all sorts of acrobatic stunts. Like Trident.

"Where have you been today?" Trident barked over his shoulder, distracted by the game.

"Trading," was all G.E. offered in explanation.

"Well, a this kid from #1384 mentioned that Saul guy you keep asking about."

"What did he say?" G.E. had been pursuing the rumor of a manager that once worked at their Supercenter. Legend had it, he was the only non-recruit to leave. But some say he didn't travel to Pepsicon. He went somewhere else.

"If you weren't messing around, you could have been here yourself," Trident said, still visibly peeved his friend had once again ducked out of training. "Anyways, he only said that the recruits in #1384 heard the story from some of the older kids a while back."

"And? What else did he say?"

"He only said the guy was supposed to be Jewish—that's some sort of religion. That was it, the chat got cut. I didn't even say anything in reply, and still I got flagged for Illicit Voice Chat. Which, I might add, would have gone on your discipline referral, had you—"

"Had I been here, I know, I know. Well, I'm here now."

Trident pointed to the enormous, bloated messenger bag slung over G.E.'s arm, filled with supplies he had gathered in anticipation of tonight's exodus. "What's with all the gear?" he asked with his bushy eyebrows furrowed.

G.E.'s folded arms tucked his skateboard to his chest. A small video camera icon flashed in the corner of the screen.

He used this as an opportunity to change the topic. "What's this new content?"

"What? That?" Trident nodded to the screen. "Probably just another recruitment advertisement."

"Maybe it's important. Finish your round and let's see."

"Roger that," Trident said. He snapped his helicopter in a tight 180 degree twist. The sudden optical shift on the giant screen strained G.E.'s eyes. As he leveled out, six enemy helicopters appeared flying at them on the screen. They let loose a flurry of rockets. Trident—his craft now drifting backward and upward—locked onto each and delivered a battery of his own hellfire rockets as the enemy rockets sped toward him. He pressed the flight yoke forward, causing his craft to arch backwards in a loop, until it hung upside-down in the sky and allowed the enemy rockets to sail neatly beneath. He turned the helicopter back over, released the yoke, and folded his hands behind his head—just in time to give his audience a view of each enemy helicopter exploding in tandem. The score flashed upon the screen and the recruits in the Electronics Department around him tentatively applauded, stunned by the performance.

After his score tallied, the video loaded. Between skirmishes, the recruits were occasionally shown promotional videos for the Virtual Training Corps. Today's at first appeared as nothing unusual. The video began with a young man about G.E.'s age, dressed in the same blue vest and standing in a perfect facsimile of his own Electronics Department. The recruit swept a flat hand to his temple and snapped it outward. G.E. rolled his eyes at the others beside him saluting the screen. He dropped down onto a couch beside Trident, rested his feet on his skateboard and rocked it left and right.

The Electronics Department background faded out and left the recruit standing before a terraced, stone edifice covered in vines. Instead of playing the game, this recruit *became* the game. A machete in hand, the intrepid recruit hacked at animated vines that sought to ensnare him as he began his ascent.

The recruit climbed the vines that spilled over each vertiginous tier, hacking all the way, until at last he reached the summit of the ancient structure. There at the peak, he found a golden, pulsating Light Rifle hovering above a white pillar. He broke into a sprint, his eye on the weapon in the distance. As he ran, his foot landed on a single stone that sank into the floor, triggering a booby-trap that spit a handful of feathered darts from a slot on a nearby wall. With a quick somersault, he just narrowly dropped below their trajectory. The recruit dove for the rifle. Upon snatching it, his uniform transformed from Buy-All blue to the green-gray camouflage of an official Army soldier. After an extra, perfunctory somersault, he leveled the rifle. Up from the corner of the edifice crawled a number of corduroy clad, long-haired Schwags—the official nemesis of the Siege Arena. His rifle fired bursts of red laser and a number in the top right of the screen counted score: 100, 250, 400.

The scene ended after the extermination of a dozen or so zombies. Next, it transitioned to a geodesic structure floating in space, the object meant to represent the structure of interconnected Buy-All Supercenters. An oblong silver rocket launched from one of the hubs, blasted toward the camera and out of frame, leaving behind its pitch:

## COMMERCE. MERCHANDISE. DEMOCRACY.
## JOIN THE VIRTUAL TRAINING CORPS

And then,

## BRING DEMOCRACY TO PEPISCON

And finally,

## THE TOURNAMENT BEGINS NEXT WEEK

Now the applause of the recruits was more jubilant. High-fives spread through their ranks. This was it, the message they had be waiting for. It had been nearly two years since the last recruitment drive. They didn't waste time making preparations. Immediately, a former recruit named Randall kicked the younger recruits from the lesser consoles to make room for those old enough for a shot at qualifying. He then plugged spare Siege Arena consoles into every available television.

Every score from this moment forward would go toward their qualifying totals. On the day of the tournament, the recruits would trade turns, competing against other recruits in other Supercenters. The battles would be every-man-for-himself, skirmishes of 2-6 players, with only the highest ranked recruits performing in one-on-one contests. The number of kills and speed in which they were obtained would generate a score. Much to G.E.'s dismay, accuracy counted for nothing, and his slow, calculating play style would put him at a disadvantage. If a recruit should amass a score of 1800 on that day, they would earn passage to Pepsicon.

G.E., however, didn't begin calculating his odds and instead cast his gaze upward at the ceiling, troubled by the spatial content of the ad. He did not know how far beyond the walls, how far the fluorescent-fixtured ceiling reached, how far one must travel before finally accessing the vastness of outer space. Consequently, such speculation was futile, but this was not what discouraged G.E. What discouraged G.E. was the other recruits' unwavering commitment to their cause. Just what was the objective? Sure, sure, the safety and liberation of the Pepsicans from the anti-capitalist tenets of Schwagism, the future prosperity of Buy-All, but how was such a thing measured? These savages, these Schwags, why did they hate Buy-All? Had they really infected the Supercenter in Aisle 39 as Benson had said? Freedom lies in the free market, Benson once said. Such questions never troubled the other recruits. They signed their recruitment contracts without breaking their gaze from the video screen of the Siege Arena. It wasn't so much that they were sold on the adventure, just that they never really put any thought into it. Time spent thinking of anything outside the competitions was time wasted.

In addition, Brett's assurance his parents would not return for G.E. troubled him. G.E. had only a vague memory of a man they called Saul, who watched over him and helped take care of Nestlé when she was just a baby. But none of the other associates knew his name, and he was forbidden to discuss the matter with Supercenterintendent Benson.

Trident changed the program to Tactical Combat and reached for his Light Rifle, hoping G.E. would stop staring at the ceiling and join in. Randall jumped in on the second position before G.E. had an opportunity. He stuffed a handful of colored jelly beans into his mouth with one hand and manipulated his Light Rifle with the other. The game began.

Trident leveled his Light Rifle and sent his animated avatar out upon the virtual landscape. G.E. looked down to find Randall's avatar aimlessly tossing grenades over an embankment as he stuffed jelly beans into his mouth.

An eight-year-old stood by the cash register in the Electronics Department. G.E. seized this opportunity to wish his closest friend good luck in the tournament.

"That's you, Randy. Go ring that kid up," G.E. said.

"What are you, my manager now? I'm kickin' butt." Randall continued throwing grenades over the embankment, hoping for the best. His numbers weren't high enough to grant him full-time competitive employ and corporate sponsorship. Consequently, he worked part time maintaining the managerless Electronics Department. This included the register. Trident swept back and forth over the artificial landscape in a helicopter. A mortar launched by the Red Team, Supercenter #1319, finally landed on Randall, ending the round.

"Dang! See what you did! You distracted me."

"Let me guess, you had them right where you wanted them?" G.E. raised an eyebrow.

"I get another turn," Randall said.

"Dammit. You're not even a recruit anymore." G.E. sighed and marched over to the cash register and logged into the machine. He took a boxed video game from the kid's hands and read the title. Blood Slayers 4.

"You can afford this?" he asked. The kid began piling old video game cartridges onto the counter.

"I'll trade these in. Just tell me how many you need."

"These are worth like a buck a piece, kid. Blood Slayers is sixty right now." G.E. began stacking the old game cartridges. "You do know you won't be able to play any of these ever again. You understand what it means to sell these back?"

"I don't care. I *need* that game." The kid was intractable, on the verge of bursting.

"You can do what you want kid. But this game will be like forty dollars next week, you know."

"I can't wait that long!" he croaked. This caught the attention of Randall.

"That game is full of suck, kid," Randall shouted.

Deprived of the gratification he sought, the kid began to cry. G.E. understood why Blood Slayers was the most popular title of the moment. The movie was released on the Buy-Net just last week. It was the story of a class of thirty primary school students who find the Education Department of their Supercenter overrun by Schwag sympathizers, a plot line that disturbingly coincided with Benson's words that afternoon. Just like in the previous three films, the evil Schwags ordered them to fight each other to the death using common Supercenter Merchandise. The idea being they would kill each other before being groomed as Virtual Training Corps recruits and shipped to the Planet Pepsicon to fight the Schwags. At no point is it ever explained how the Schwags found their way across the galaxy to invade their Supercenter. The film wastes no time and essentially amounts to ninety solid minutes of gore-drenched gladiatorial combat with common Supercenter items used as cudgels. Brooms, staplers, curtain rods, picture frames, extension cords. A rubber mallet. In the end, the one surviving kid winds up impaling the lead Schwag sympathizer with a shattered fluorescent light bulb that somehow still holds a charge and sets his head on fire.

G.E. reluctantly rang the kid up.

"You know," he added as he swiped the kid's associate badge, "when I was your age we were playing Mario games. What ever happened to that?" The kid gave him a look of utter contempt.

"That game sucks." He slowly articulated his words, contemptuous of the entire canon of classic platform games. "Maybe you should play Mario games. I saw what you did the other day. You ran away from the Red Team like a little bitch."

"Like a what? Where does a kid your age even learn words like that?"

"You heard me, bitch."

"Okay, now you are freaking me out and making it sound ridiculous. Besides, if anybody here is a little bitch—you know, forget it. What are you even talking about?" The kid had succeeded in intimidating G.E., or at least confounding him. He remembered the match the kid referred to. His entire Blue Squad had been killed in a well-placed ambush and he, cautiously following up the rear, was the last man standing, though badly injured. Most recruits would just give up at that point, run into the enemy, guns blazing and grenades flying, fully expecting to get killed. "Rambo," they called it, and quickly ending the match was seen as proper etiquette when the odds were stacked that badly against you. But G.E. never ran Rambo. Not then, not ever.

The kid explained, "You ran away from that ambush—"

"Yeah, to pick up a health pack!"

"Like a scared little bitch."

G.E. groaned with frustration. "Like the guy who wound up winning the match! Keep in mind, opponents outnumbered me six to one!"

"Why didn't you just throw a grenade into that bunker?"

"And kill myself in the process?"

"You'd get six kills, easy, win the round."

"And if I got only five? I lose. You can't rely on grenades like that."

"'Nade have been cooler," the kid said as he walked away.

G.E. logged off the cash register, grabbed his skateboard, and left the Electronics Department. He allayed his frustration, remembering that in just a few short hours, upon nightfall, he would leave the Supercenter once and for all.

# CHAPTER 3

➲ **Education**

When he arrived at the Education Department to pick up his sister, G.E. noticed the children had strung up a banner of construction paper Buy-All smiley faces, each with a letter of the alphabet printed neatly upon the sheet in crayon. This created a playful sort of entryway into the department and distinguished it from the more traditional retail departments. Despite their best efforts to differentiate, the Educational Department itself was composed of little more than a dozen or so kiosks that occupied the Boys and Girls Wear Department. Children sat on mats, in rings around circular clothing racks relieved of garments, the shiny steel racks converted to Educational Kiosks and outfitted with television monitors and DVD players. Some included practice pricing guns and dummy cash registers for training youth too uncoordinated to manage the Siege Arena Gaming System.

Early on in their lives, around the age of six, the children were separated into two groups. First, those with the Motor Coordinal Potential to thrive in the Siege Arena. Second, those not demonstrating this promise. This latter group would be left to occupy menial positions around the Supercenter. Children's games for this group involved shelving and stocking, adding and subtracting. An area in the back of the Education Department was designated for Physical Routine. In the small corral, a handful of kids raced around with brooms, chasing a bevy of packing peanuts. Others carefully placed a collection of odd-sized empty boxes into a tall practice shelf, meticulously shelving and unshelving them like puzzle pieces.

The school's Education Facilitator, Supercenterintendent Edward Benson, stepped away from the central information kiosk to give G.E. a disapproving scowl. G.E.'s heart skipped a beat, but it was way too soon for Benson to have received word of his visit to Aisle 39. He reassured himself this was Benson's typical expression, most anytime he saw G.E. or anyone else for that matter.

"After what you did today," Benson said. "After our little talk. I falsely presumed we would see an uptick in your behavior. But then, trespassing into Aisle 39? A strictly off-limits area?"

G.E. shook his head. The security orbs truly watched everything, at all times. Still, he couldn't quite muster the confidence to tell his former teacher to get fragged.

"I just had to check on something," he said at last. He mentally kicked himself for not preparing an excuse.

Benson narrowed his eyes.

"There is nothing for you in that place. Those people..." he chose his words carefully, "they are becoming *Schwags*."

"What?" This startled G.E. "Like the ones we are fighting? On Pepsicon?"

"Quiet!" Benson whispered. This was a risky gambit, but he was happy to see it find traction in the young recruit's mind. "Now you can see why the war effort is so important?"

"But—" G.E. began again, a thousand questions flooding his mind.

"Listen, Mr. Westinghouse," the Supercenterintendent cut him off. "Your number one priority at this juncture lies with the upcoming tournament. Not with the treasonous antics of those miscreants."

"If they are really Schwags, how do you know? Have you been to Pepsicon? Have you seen one for yourself?"

"Yes." Benson's expression grew suddenly grave. He swallowed hard before continuing. "I've seen them alright.... I remember it well...." His eyes darted around the ceiling. "Begging for change, barefoot.... Rolling their own cigarettes...." He remained distant for a moment, and then snapped himself out of it. "Do you understand me, boy?" Benson asked sternly. "Do you feel you have adequately prepared for this tournament?"

G.E. swallowed hard. "Yes, sir."

"You will be facing the top recruits of other Supercenters. And you will do something about that hair of yours before Sergeant Hildebrand has a chance to see how far you've lapsed into insubordination."

"I know, sir. Yessir."

"This doesn't seem to worry you?"

"I will win."

"We shall see then, won't we?"

G.E. said nothing more, but he was certain of victory. He had already devised a foolproof plan. One victory was all he needed, and considering this would be his last battle, he intended to play his one trump card. It would only work once.

Eight children wore headphones and sat crossed-legged

around the kiosk beside Benson. They watched a small video screen. A full day of watching video with little opportunity to exercise was no small feat, but aided by the stimulant *Attencizin*, most kids could stick it out without growing too restless. Today's lesson was History. Just as G.E. had only six years prior, the children learned only the mission-critical parts of history. The company's founding in 1962, incorporation, the initial public offering, the day it became the world's largest private employer. Crude, sometimes confusing edits ensured all the scenes were interior, as Management didn't allow mentions of an outside world within the walls of the Supercenter. Some of the changes were mundane, some imperceptible, and others almost silly. Such as Second Sunday. Years of Buy-All productivity analysis proved that Mondays were indeed the most morose day of the week. But Monday just had a bad rap. So they were done away with in favor of Second Sunday.

Not all the Buy-Alls were closed Supercenters like #1501. At that same moment, a pregnant, single mother in a Buy-All on the Eastern seaboard, and north of the Potomac River, where war didn't rage, where Buy-All Supercenters hadn't sealed their doors and agreed to participate in this social experiment, came upon an odd advertisement in a plastic frame, beside the Employee of the Month placards and the fire code documentation, a small advertisement notifying expecting mothers of Buy-All's participation in a not-for-profit adoption program. She would not suspect anything like this the result of such philanthropy—that these infants wound up in corporate nurseries and eventually distributed to sealed Buy-All Supercenters in the Midwest.

G.E. felt something tug at the corner of his vest and shake him from his wandering thoughts of Schwag ideology infiltrating associates of the Supercenter. He looked down to find his little sister, Nestlé, rubbing her eyes with fists.

Nestlé was only ten years old, thin but spry, with thick, wavy blond hair framing an ever-curious expression, despite looking a bit bleary and tired as she stood beside her brother. After a six-hour day of educational videos and more or less educational video games, coming home from school was like waking from a long nap. Next year, she would graduate from primary school, at which point the Supercenterintendent would assign her to either the Siege Arena or Customer Service. G.E. resented either outcome. He tucked his skateboard under his arm, took his little sister's hand and began the walk back to their bunk on Aisle 17.

Their path took them through the most congested aisles of the Supercenter, packed with associates browsing merchandise or going about their off-duty errands. On-duty associates ran floor buffers, others hauled cartloads of garbage, bound for a large metal chute in the Merchandise Room, the depths of which were unknown. Others congregated around large-screen televisions broadcasting either war updates from the Planet Pepsicon, situational comedies set on the Planet Pepsicon, or Siege Arena highlights and commentary. At the moment G.E. and Nestlé passed by the Electronics Department, a highlight reel played on an array of two dozen variable sized televisions. He tried not to look, but the sight of the digitized face of his gaming avatar gave momentary pause. Once his sister saw it, he couldn't pull her away.

"Hey, Gee!" Nestlé shouted. "That's your guy!" The

novelty hadn't worn off. Four-hundred and twenty-eight Buy-Alls across the country hosted Siege Arena teams, squadrons of roughly 14 recruits each. In the last year since G.E. resolved to earn passage to Pepsicon, his name became an increasingly common sight upon the leader boards and, consequently, highlight shows like this. The televisions played a popular Siege Arena highlight show called "Inside the Bunker." The program featured little more than shouting matches between three talking heads, guaranteed to play contrarian to one another.

"G.E. Westinghouse," the burly, deep-voiced one in the center began after a few clips aired. "Here's a real contender, coming out this season, eligible for Pepsicon—"

"But I'm not seeing much fight in this fish," said the mullet-wearing commentator to his left. But before he could continue, the third cut him off.

"I'm calling it now—this season's top tactical combat player." He slammed his palm on the desk before him. "1501's G.E. Westinghouse. Mark it down."

"Oh come on!" said the first. "Please! Running around and plinking off headshots is no way to—"

"Top rankings," the third commentator interjected, "in both kill count and time to completion. Both deadly and efficient."

"But where's the heart?" said the mullet.

"And," the first continued, "when have you seen a sniper-class take a title—any title. Fact is, this is a lack of maturity at best, a cynical exploit at worst!"

"Are you calling him a cheater?" asked the third, perhaps only obligatorily advocating for G.E.

"Of course not! An exploit merely makes the most out of a given situation, takes advantage of the arena's gaming mechanics themselves. Seeks out and finds weakness in the programming—"

"Bad sportsmanship," the mullet added before the first could continue.

"—Precisely. The Siege Arena was meant to test close-range, small-arms fire. Sure, you can go around zapping the enemy at 400 meters and then run for cover, but the real point is submachine gun—"

"Then why have a sniper class at all!" said the third.

"One of many tactics but not the only—"

"G.E. has 1400 hours logged as a Demolition-class, 6300 surface-to-air kills—"

"Sniper's evil twin—" tagged the mullet.

"Oh come on!" the others said in unison.

With that, their voices muddled together in argument.

G.E. took the opportunity to walk away from the Electronics Department, towing his awestruck sister along by her hand. Together, they moved on through the center aisle of the Supercenter, named just that—Center Aisle—where the largest merchandise resided. Within Center Aisle, an associate could find communal furniture, big-screen televisions, video game systems, an inflatable vinyl play castle for the youngest children, and other remnants from the pre-closure era, items left behind by the rampant looting that occurred on the day of the Closure. The assorted chairs, couches, and tables formed a gathering area. Off-duty associates were permitted to enjoy this furniture at their leisure. As if the access to state-of-the-art video game systems was not enough,

Center Aisle was a regular Funland. Board games, Sudoku puzzles, and hand-held video game systems littered the tables along with copies of the Supercenter News. Most spectacular of all, however, were the free samples.

"Can we stop at the concession stand?" Nestlé asked, clapping her small hands together and grinning. G.E. rolled his eyes, aggravated by his sister's tone that somehow implied this was not an everyday occurrence. Each time Nestlé proposed stopping for a free sample, she did so as though this were a novel idea she'd never before conceived. At least there was one good reason to stop—it was Second Sunday, it was Candy Day.

Buster, the concession attendant, plunged a large plastic scoop into a basket filled with rubbery, purple candy bears. He delicately filled a tiny paper cup with the treats and handed it to G.E., who tossed the entirety of its contents into his mouth. Buster knelt down to Nestlé and gestured toward an array of identical baskets, each brimming with a rainbow of colored treats.

"Any color you'd like, little darlin'," he added with a soothing cowboy drawl.

Associates pawed through nearby bins of plastic pouches, evaluating their selection carefully, as any prudent shopper should. Grape, Orange, Cherry, Pineapple, Strawberry—G.E. knew these flavors well, but made no connection to actual fruit itself. Like the others, he assumed that the terms had originated with Yummy Bear brand gelatinized confectionery and simply described the particular set of laboratory-made ester tastes—sweet, tangy, and sour.

While Center Aisle offered a model portrait of Buy-All, aisles that stretched in either direction grew increasingly less ideal. Some departments had grown obsolete and were subsequently neglected. Aisles that were no long shopped saw their shelves stripped of merchandise. Some aisles had been converted to housing compartments, but more often abandoned outright. G.E. learned at a young age that some aisles, not the least of which included Aisle 39, you simply don't walk down.

But Aisle 17 was only two aisles away from Center Aisle and, thankfully, one of the better neighborhoods in the Supercenter. Once he was officially recognized as a Siege Arena recruit, he and Nestlé were moved far away from Aisle 39, to Aisle 17, where many of the other recruits were housed. G.E. and Nestlé's home was located in packing and office supplies. Curtains were drawn over the higher shelves, reserved as Department Compartments, simple living quarters. Ladders ran down these shelves to the floor. Today, their neighbor, Huck, sat in a folding lawn chair, passing time as other guest associates meandered about, picking up a pair of scissors or a magic marker here and there. Just shopping. Idle shopping.

They climbed the ladder up to their compartment, a compartment identical to all the others of the aisle, save a strange red blotch of old paint on the shelf beam. G.E. never could figure out why it was there and often wondered if it meant something.

The compartment G.E. and Nestlé shared was an eight-by-three shelf, walled with white pegboard decorated with the watercolor and finger paint artwork of Nestlé. Her choice canvas was white construction paper, on which she captured her favorite subject: stars, planets, meteoroids, spaceships. Like her older brother, the virtual worlds they inhabited within electronic gaming systems captivated her. G.E. often thought that if Nestlé ever had a chance to compete in the Siege Arena she'd just spend the whole time looking up at the stars, undisturbed by the combat raging all around her.

Empty snack wrappers, clothing, stuffed animals, and assorted hand-held video game cartridges littered the metal floor of their compartment. On the far wall, as was the case with every other compartment, their own personal computer connected them, at all times, to the Buy-Net. A pair of bean-bag chairs separated the computer viewing side of the compartment from the sleeping area—side-by-side sleeping bags on inflatable camping mattresses.

Nestlé stuffed her hand in an open box of breakfast cereal and filled her mouth with crunchy bits of puffed corn and marshmallow. Due to logistical constraints, food and merchandise were delivered monthly. Perishable goods were an impossibility. Staples such as milk, eggs, meat, and bread were completely unheard of among Buy-All Supercenters. The associates encountered meat only in the maligned form of beef jerky, but very few associates developed a fondness for nitrated sheets of ruby sirloin. After a few handfuls of cereal, Nestlé picked up her hand-held Mini-Siege gaming device and began thumbing through a stack of thin plastic cartridges.

"How was school?" G.E. asked, trying to get his mind off the brass key burning in his breast pocket.

Nestlé yawned and shrugged her shoulders. She tossed the handful of tiny plastic cartridges back to the floor of the compartment. This was how they spent their evenings, now for the past ten years, trying to keep the constant bombardment of electronic stimuli afloat, stuff down some snacks for dinner, maybe watch some television until they fell asleep.

Then Nestlé would dream of far-away planets, twinkling stars, sparkling comets—the accumulated psychic minutia of video game media blended with her own wildly inventive and awestruck imagination. G.E., however, dreamt only of the Merchandise Machine, a labyrinthine network of twisting silver conduits, modular scaffolding, and iron latticework that reached into impossible, infinite, circular depths, where up and down, top and bottom, became obsolete. Recently, the dreams had grown far more intense than ever. The only remedy, he reasoned, was a glance, just one simple glance, into the room beyond the Shuttle Bay door. Or perhaps just a little past that.

"Listen, Nestlé. Something came up." G.E. squeezed the brass key in his pocket.

"Do you mean the tournament?" Nestlé asked. This was the last thing on G.E.'s mind.

"No, not really...."

"Are you going to play in it?" Nestlé asked as she turned her attention away from the Mini-Siege game and to her collection of finger paints.

"Compete, Nestlé. We're not just playing games."

"What's the difference?" She blinked. G.E. saw she wasn't being sarcastic. He took a deep breath to calm his frustration before continuing. He thought about explaining all the subtle nuances of competitive tactical combat, but it really just came down to one difference.

"When you are playing, you are at least having fun."

Nestlé thought about this for a moment as she struggled to unscrew the cap on her canister of black paint.

"Then why are you doing it?"

"I guess it is a way out of the Supercenter." G.E. took the can from her and broke the seal of dried paint.

She gasped. "Are you going to Pepsicon?" Her eyes widened and thoughts of losing her brother took hold. Nestlé didn't know much about the war on Pepsicon, only that every aspect of associate life was a shared sacrifice on behalf of obtaining victory. And among those associates of Buy-All Supercenter #1501, this sense of imminent peril manifested itself in many ways. In G.E., it fostered restlessness. An indefinable claustrophobia, concentration, and dexterity in Trident. And, in Nestlé, elaborate and surreal paintings.

"I don't know exactly, but one thing I'm certain of—I promise not to leave you behind," G.E. said. He handed the can of paint to her and put his hand on her head. He would insist she came along. They would probably tell him no. In this event, he would refuse passage. Now that he'd seen the HVAC Schematic, he knew for sure there was another way out. There had to be.

Nestlé took these words in stride, G.E. expected as much. She had no conception of any place beyond the Supercenter. *Matter of fact*, G.E. thought, *neither do I*. He turned on the Buy-Net computer terminal and began reading reviews on flashlights, presuming darkness lay beyond the Supercenter after having once peeked through the crack at the base of the Shuttle Bay door. Nestlé soon abandoned her gaming system and, as she inevitably did, instead set down to painting.

Before long, her face and arms were blotched in a black leopard pattern, her hands gloved in thick, greasy finger paint. Nestlé created another wavy, impressionistic rendering of outer space, as she had witnessed through the medium of video games. She covered the white paper entirely in black finger paint and then carefully layered yellow stars of various sizes.

"You're going to wind up falling into one of those paintings," G.E. said gesturing to her face and arms. Nestlé looked at her arms, noticing only then what a mess she had made of the entire compartment. She nodded at the mess, first with amazement, then satisfaction.

"Fall into a painting...." she repeated, enamored by the thought. G.E. waited for this moment of reverie to pass and then helped her tack it to an open space on their pegboard compartment wall.

"So where's the Supercenter?" he asked as he dropped into a blue beanbag chair.

She bent her head to look, studied her painting for a moment, and then pointed between two stars in the top corner.

"Somewhere back there," she said confidently.

G.E. studied the black swirls and found them a soothing map of the universe. He leaned back in the beanbag chair and took in the painting. She had gone through four cans of finger paint turning her canvas black. The vastness of space immediately overwhelmed him. As G.E. stared into the painting, his eyes fell out of focus. The edges of the golden stars flickered and burned. Within these thick, wavy swirls of black, his imagination soared. His thoughts stretched further than the farthest boundaries of the Siege Arena battleground, forever masked in a fog of blackness and no true place at all.

His memory was a fog of blackness as well. Not in space, but time. The further back he remembered, the blacker his recollection. He scarcely remembered the day the soldiers filled the Supercenter. He was only six years old, Nestlé just a baby. His sole preoccupation that morning was playing with a plastic cement mixer, stuffing tiny pieces of candy into the tumbler, rolling it around three times before shaking them out to eat. He remembered his mother with tears in her eyes, fighting the soldiers. The soldiers tried very hard to console her and begged her to calm down. G.E. remembered his father leaning down to him. Each year it became harder, not to remember his words, but harder to remain certain. The parents walked through the Shuttle Bay doors in single file. His father, just before he turned to leave, spoke to him.

"We are going for help. We are going to find help and then we'll be back." If not these exact words, G.E. was at least certain of his father's promise to return.

As the Army men kept watch over him and Nestlé, a piece of candy became lost in the inner gears of the cement mixer and G.E. could not shake it free. It rattled and rattled, but would not fall out. A soldier offered him another roll of candies, but this was no solace. The soldiers passed around the toy truck, tried to free the candy from the toy as G.E. wailed. This was the last of his memory. He never found out what happened to that tiny plastic cement mixer.

The colorful swirls of his sister's painting fell into blurry focus as tears filled his eyes.

"Another masterpiece," G.E. said as he recovered. He looked around the compartment, his heart aching in his chest. "Now let's get you cleaned up."

# CHAPTER 4

➡ **Pharmaceutical**

**Artificial Night. At 8:00 p.m.,** the lights dimmed, as they did each day, to promote a healthy circadian rhythm among the associates. Many slept during the dim hours, the world outside the walls of the Supercenter coincidentally dark as well. However, a skeleton crew of associates tended merchandise. This was, after all, a 24-hour Supercenter. But few associates perused the aisles during these late-night hours. The long row of cash registers serving as a boundary between the greater retail environment and the scarified threshold sealed them off from the outdoor world. Each register lay dormant, save one. At the far end, a bleary-eyed cashier drew merchandise across the bar code scanning table between her and the first customer in the last three hours.

Her customer at this late hour was one among Aisle 39's elite. A disaffected unassociate named Keith squinted, said nothing, and swiped an associate badge to finalize his transaction. She did not check to see that the photo on the badge matched—it didn't. The ID badge was one of several obtained by Brett, the forfeited badges of unassociates likely unaware their meager credit accounts were being drained for this purpose.

She finished loading the cart, half-mumbled the total, and stuffed the receipt in one of the dozen blue, plastic bags.

Keith rolled the heavily laden shopping cart away from the cashier. Glancing surreptitiously at the passing aisles, he threw a blanket over the cart to further conceal its contents. With few other associates in sight, he crept slowly down the sanguine Center Aisle at midnight, stealing glances at other night shift associates, shuffling somnambulists pushing dust brooms and whirring floor buffers about the empty aisles.

The grim unassociate wheeled the cart to Aisle 39. His face was pinched and sullen, and long black bangs hung just over his eyebrows. Keith suffered from a severe food allergy to nuts. A childhood sans protein had left him with thin hair, blanched skin, and remarkably bad posture. Of the many unassociates joining Brett in his provisional arcade den, Keith possessed an underlying acrimonious current, not only toward Management, but humanity in general. He pressed onward, to Aisle 39, where he had claimed a home shelf ever since his untimely wash-out from the Siege Arena and subsequent assignment to Inventory Control.

Though Keith purchased this same combination of unusual items several times before, never once had he attempted such a large quantity. Just as before, the cashier didn't question what he may do with four boxes of gallon-sized, resealable freezer bags, six quarts of fingernail polish remover, a gallon of ammonia, powdered lemonade drink mix, and, most notably, four dozen bottles of cough syrup.

This was the merchandise Keith revealed to the sentries standing guard outside of Aisle 39. One sentry lifted the corner of the blanket from the cart with his curtain rod.

"Somebody sick?" he asked as he drew aside the large quilt that draped before the threshold and allowed Keith to pass. The concoction Keith hoped to conjure that evening had been nicknamed "tile melt" by the unassociates because of its tendency to produce visual hallucinations that invariably created an impression of the Supercenter floor bending and flowing in ribbons of alternating, serried layers, as if melting.

Keith looked down and pressed the heavy cart through, pausing at the last second to whisper to the sentry, "Brett says everybody sick."

Keith wheeled his cart past several UAC revolutionaries, hand-copying a pamphlet titled "The Wealth of Departments" for circulation among the other associates. This manuscript outlined the UAC's overarching agenda and theory of labor distribution as it pertained to customer service representatives, stockers, janitorial custodians, and cashiers. Management positions were given cursory regard, and only as archaic, obsolete, parasitic, sinecures that would be eliminated at once, should the Supercenter move upon a collective bargaining agreement. Among several ideas outlined in this manifesto, the most pressing was the charge to end the 40-hour work week, which the UAC decried as utter servitude.

At last he reached Aisle 39, where he found Brett resting in a plastic deck lounger, thick black sunglasses covering his eyes, his gaming alcove lit at night with long fluorescent black lights. When he saw Keith, he lifted a small eye-dropper bottle that held about an ounce of cloudy yellow liquid.

He tilted the tiny bottle to the ceiling and offered a toast. "To Freedom."

He squeezed the tiny vial into his mouth. The others grunted and clapped lightly in approval. Upon the floor, Brett had assembled a crude laboratory—several empty water jugs, into which he mixed his ingredients. He passed out bottles of cough syrup to the other unassociates around him as he explained.

"Mix, shake, separate, pour. That's all there is to it."

Had the associates of Buy-All #1501 a simple cup of orange juice, perhaps a week-old bowl of oatmeal, and had the air-circulation system allowed microscopic yeast to enter from the outside world, then perhaps at one time over the last ten years some associate may have discovered by accident the ethanol byproduct of yeast metabolism. But there was no juice. There was no oatmeal. There was no microorganism. Powdered orange drink mix and bits of rolled oats bound by high-fructose corn syrup in the form of granola bars were plentiful, but, alas, impervious to yeast.

The unassociates watched with curiosity as Brett mixed and moved quantities of liquid back and forth between these crude beakers. The cough syrup glowed with yellow phosphorescence in the ultraviolet light.

"Pay attention, now," Brett explained, "Only one ingredient in the syrup is psychoactive. Lucky for us, it's also the only ingredient that will go into a non-polar solution."

He added a vial of cough medicine to a jug of fingernail polish remover. The other unassociates winced at the acrid odor. When he added drain cleaner, the fingernail polish remover turned pink and floated on top of the cough syrup. Brett then added the mix to a resealable freezer bag. He fastened the bag to an alligator clip and, after a few minutes, the liquid separated. Brett then snipped the corner and drained the bottom layer into a waste bottle, the top layer into a Pyrex casserole dish. The fingernail polish remover would soon evaporate away to leave a crusty white film, which could be dissolved in super-concentrated powdered lemonade drink mix to help cover the astringent taste.

Tiny vials of Tile Melt found their way into associate hands through the UAC's careful and clandestine dispense. Brett insisted that only associates over the age of 13 were permitted, though he knew this would be impossible to enforce. He credited Management with the responsibility of policing the Supercenter. After all, if they were so concerned, then maybe they would re-open the Supercenter and call off this mad experiment altogether.

Tile Melt dissociated one from the familiar, and nothing was more familiar than their individual conscious selves, which Tile Melt fractured and dissolved. Painfully familiar, utterly routine tasks became a mind-boggling impossibility. Ordinarily, the tile floor was swept, reswept, mopped, buffed, and rebuffed. Products were counted and measured, prices marked up and prices marked down, returns repackaged and reshelved. But upon availing themselves of this chemical inebriant, the associates simply marveled at the void, the absence left in the inebriated stupor of Tile Melt. Their routines became obsolete and, for a few hours, they neither serviced nor shopped merchandise, but existed as if for the first time in their lives, separate and apart from it.

Knowing the upcoming tournament would lead to Sergeant Hildebrand's untimely return to the Supercenter, Brett planned to place the associates of Buy-All Supercenter #1501 into a delicate slumber from which they would not soon wake.

One associate awake at this late hour was neither on duty

as an associate nor indulging in the dissociative effects of Tile Melt.

One G.E. Westinghouse stood outside the Shuttle Bay door, alone with no one else in sight. A backpack slung over his shoulder, skateboard under his arm, he looked left, right, and, from the breast pocket of his associate vest, produced the solitary brass key Brett gave him that afternoon.

G.E. took a deep breath and prepared himself for the unknown depths that lie beyond the Shuttle Bay doors. *I'm just going out for a little recon*, he assured himself. *Once I get into the next Supercenter, I come back for Nestlé.* He pressed the key to the keyhole—but it didn't fit. It didn't even kind of fit.

Brett had traded him a counterfeit key for his counterfeit MP3 players.

# CHAPTER 5

 Security

**Within his secretive office, G.M.** Sam Torino sat in his leather executive chair, black and white security monitors stacked floor-to-ceiling on the wall behind him. He kept the light in his office dim at all times to aid in the scrutiny of these monitors. A tiny, miniaturization of a man, he sat in a normal-sized office chair, raised to maximum height to give him just enough clearance over the top of his desk to see any visitor, provided that visitor remain standing. Primordial dwarfism left him standing only three feet tall, though his build was perfectly proportional. He had light, wispy brown hair combed in a pompadour, adding a small but ultimately significant bonus to his height. The G.M. would be wearing his usual hopeful, earnest expression—provided nothing were amiss with his Supercenter, but as of late, this was seldom the case.

With his Supercenterintendent standing before him, Torino brooded over the evil specter of dissent. Shiftless unassociates congregated in the former Automotive Department, going so far as to physically commandeer and, as they called it, "occupy" an entire aisle to themselves as a zealous form of protest—Aisle 39. For years these destitute aisles served as a sober example of beleaguering poverty, and this helped keep the other associates in line, but now they had devised a new, insidious means to attract associates to their cause.

"Explain to me how a chemical intoxicant has found its way into this Supercenter," Torino said, his voice a bit soprano, yet stern and authoritative.

"We have no reason to believe such a thing has occurred. I've had our Merchandise Lead pore over every palette, open every box and search every container. We've found no evidence of contraband."

"Then we must conclude it is somehow manufactured here in the store."

Benson guffawed. "Impossible. Without proper access to laboratory facilities, let alone compositions and things with... molecular structures."

"For all your condescension, you too often underestimate the ingenuity of retail workers seeking inebriation. I have reason to believe Aisle 39 is behind this."

Benson's eyes darted from monitor to monitor. Torino placed both his hands at the corner of his desk and slung his chair around to face the monitors. "You were not with us at the time," he said, "but there was once a children's toy that contained a dangerous narcotic. Innocuous little colored beads. All it took was some poor toddler swallowing a bunch of them and falling into a coma. The parents had no idea what happened. But the children knew. You could see the secret turning in their dark little dilated eyes. Oh yes they knew. They knew the kid had eaten the beads, but they kept their little traps shut. It was only a matter of time before they began...experimenting. Word spread through the Kindergarten first. Beads vanished from the toy bins. Next came a black market, the bead-making toy flew off the shelves. Parents never understood how such a toy could become so popular. First and second graders began trading them for milk money.

"Entire elementary schools fell under its spell before anyone discovered the root cause. We may have never figured it out had a few of them not started vomiting them up intact. Thank God we got to them before the high schoolers." Torino shook his head. "The point is, these children never had the *notion* of getting high. Until the idea was planted in their nappy little heads." Torino turned in his chair to face the wall of security monitors. "At least we sold a lot of bead-making toys."

Benson's face turned pale. "They are getting stronger," he whispered. "I feel it. Something sinister dwells within Aisle 39, something more powerful, more treasonous than your former Electronics Department manager."

"Pish posh. We shall get to the bottom of this. I've busted up my own fair share of attempts at organized labor. This is nothing a good round of sales incentive programs can't fix. But first we must cut off their supply of this drug. Did you bring with you the product manifests? Are there any irregularities with sales?"

"I have the inventory records right here." Benson produced a thick folder of pink carbon forms. "Nothing unusual."

"What about Pharmaceutical?"

"Well, that's classified."

"No, no. I mean over-the-counter stuff."

"Classified."

"What? That can't be. Let me see."

Benson hurriedly flipped through the manila folder. He produced the pink carbon copy of the Merchandise Delivery

Manifest for the Pharmaceutical Department. Each line had been carefully run through with a black magic marker.

"This isn't classification, you dolt, it's a cover up!" Torino took an endless breath. "Then we have no choice," Torino said fatalistically. "We must consult The Handbook."

Torino leaned over the edge of his desk, pulled open a drawer, and drug the great binder, the Manager's Handbook, onto his desk. He kneeled before it, flipped through the contents until at last arriving at a document titled A MANAGER'S TOOLBOX FOR REMAINING DRUG FREE. He skimmed the Morale Self-Assessment Questionnaire, reading parts aloud to Benson.

"Let's see...value of teamwork, yes, we do of course value teamwork. Management open door...continuing to seek feedback from associates...fostering a partnership environment and following up with....yes, yes we do all that. And here's a bit about capitalizing on the objectives of responsible team effectiveness..." He stopped scanning the text, clapped his hands down on the pages, and groaned. "This is all just horse-hockey!"

Torino stood up and kicked the binder. It hardly budged. The information was printed prior to the Closure and severely out of date, if not out of touch with the reality of his management predicament. Responsibility for the day-to-day operations of any given Supercenter was left entirely to the General Managers. Torino was powerless to throw dissenters out of the Supercenter.

"We are already on thin ice with Hildebrand as it is," he said. "If any of our young soldiers succumb to this drug, they'll turn us into a munitions Supercenter."

"There won't be anybody to build the munitions if we don't put a stop to this," Benson added. "Tile Melt and Aisle 39. Together, they'll overrun us."

"That's preposterous."

"I saw one beating on the bottom of a paint bucket."

"What's that supposed to mean?"

"Paint buckets first. Next thing you know, they are stringing up guitars, kicking around hacky sacks."

"Mr. Benson, please."

"Our enemies walk among us."

"Our enemies walk on the Planet Pepsicon—that's all you need to know. This Supercenter is in no danger. We will ship the troublemakers out. Case in point. Your most loyal and trusted recruit." Torino reached for his remote. The wall of monitors behind him switched from their remote CCTV feeds to a pre-recorded security video.

With the infrared enabled, the picture was awash in a greenish soup, but the faces were unmistakable. The monitor revealed footage of G.E. standing at the threshold of Aisle 39. Just before he vanished behind the tarp obscuring the aisle, he paused to flash a thumbs-up to the security orb above.

Benson balled his fists. "How could he do this to us?" he cried. "That sarcastic little brat!"

"Let me make one thing clear," Torino cleared his throat. "Now, we cannot abide trouble makers. Should this brand of insolence spread, it will threaten the integrity of the recruitment program and that is something this Supercenter cannot endure. We are here for the express purpose of grooming soldiers, is that clear?"

Torino took off his tiny glasses and rubbed his eyes with

the heels of his hands.

"He tells me that he plans on competing in the tournament," Benson offered. "Seems pretty confident of victory."

"Well thank goodness for that, at least." Torino sighed and leaned back in his chair. "It is essential we keep him on our side. Back when I was an associate manager your age, I had nothing but associates just like him. Nothing but miscreants and punks. Buy-All made every concession in order to accommodate them. And how did they repay us? Skipping work, long breaks. Shrinkage. Do you understand what that term means, Benson?"

"Something to do with the natural logarithm of associate retainage over time..." Benson fumbled.

"It means stealing! They would steal! From us! And we'd just look the other way, but that wasn't enough. Still they'd up and quit without any warning or reason. In my Supercenter! *My* Supercenter!" To demonstrate his conviction, Torino stood on his chair, climbed on his desk and marched to the far side. With an index finger extended, he continued. "Do you have any idea what our recruitment numbers are?"

"No sir," Benson replied.

"Fourteen! We are expected to have groomed fully half of this year's class for deployment." Torino clasped his tiny hands behind his back and paced back and forth across his desk.

"We must show G.E. that Buy-All means business."

# CHAPTER 6

**Clean Up on Aisle 39**

**As G.E. skated to Brett's** den within Aisle 39, he found a large crowd of associates congregated outside the threshold, as if drawn by some unheard calling. There they traded in their associate IDs and all the credit within their associate accounts, for a daily allotment of Tile Melt. Glassy-eyed unassociates lay on barren shelves beside them, snoozing, engaging in political discourse, or, more often, staring at the tile floor for hours on end, as patterns danced and scintillated before their eyes, a result of having availed themselves of the popular drug.

A spontaneous artistry emerged on the barren shelves surrounding Aisle 39. The old pricing placards, promising price roll-backs on products that no longer existed, had been cryptically repainted, the smiley face given fangs, talons, scales. Others ignored the original content entirely and instead marked the signage with crude petroglyphs, stick-figures of horned human beings pushing what G.E. presumed were floor polishers.

In the open space directly before Aisle 39, G.E. discovered an unusual shrine of colored lights. Several unassociates had carefully arranged a ring of green glow sticks, LED votives, three lava lamps, and a small disco ball with a spotlight. At the center, a round globe of luminous fiber optic filaments. The entire effigy was wrapped in a ring of Christmas lights. Around this, unassociates beat out a rhythm on plastic buckets while others danced.

G.E. pressed his way past the sentries standing guard outside Aisle 39, beyond a pair of unassociates carefully binding pamphlets titled "Wage Equity and You" with a stapler not quite fit for the task, past a frighteningly makeshift chemistry apparatus, at last reaching Brett. The former Electronics Department manager busied himself repairing a pinball machine, the topglass removed.

"Bogus All-Pod players," Brett said as he wrapped a thick rubber band around a bumper rail. "That was awfully clever. I didn't see it coming, to be honest." Brett jabbed an old screwdriver into a ball ejector to free a trapped ball.

"I want the key," G.E. demanded. "The real key. I need to see what is on the other side of the Shuttle Bay."

"Smart enough to try and pull a fast one on me, but naïve enough to presume I had a way to let myself out of this prison."

"What's a prison?" G.E. asked as he folded his arms.

Brett stepped away from the pinball machine, snatched a stray bean-bag animal from the floor. He then reached for one of the milk crates repurposed as seating within Aisle 39. He tucked the bear under the crate and pressed upon it with his foot.

"That—" he grimaced as he pressed with his foot. Brett lifted himself upon it until he was at last standing and the plastic began to bend. "—is a prison."

G.E.'s brow knotted. "So there is no way out?"

"The only person with a key to this Supercenter is Sergeant Hildebrand. And he hasn't set foot in this place for almost six years. Assuming they haven't changed the goddamn clocks." Brett let himself fall into a tattered lawn chair, becoming suddenly preoccupied with his last statement. "I mean, who's to say a day is a day anymore? Who's to say they couldn't change the duration of time itself? Replace all the clocks with ones that incrementally slow down. Over time we would adjust, we wouldn't even notice the clocks were moving too slow. We might have been here for several more years than they are telling us." Brett extended his index fingers and drew them apart to demonstrate this attenuation of time. "This place may be a sort of time machine."

The preposterousness of Brett's thought process gave G.E. pause. He examined Brett's eyes, only to find them glazed, pupils enlarged, like many of the unassociates outside the aisle.

Brett took note of this, but had no intention of hiding his inebriation. He opened a cracked plastic cooler beside his chair, its Styrofoam guts bulging from the broken shell. Inside, G.E. could see dozens of tiny plastic eyedropper vials. Brett delicately removed one of these and proceeded to squirt the entire contents of a vial into his open mouth. He then tossed the empty vial over his shoulder where it nearly fell into a waste basket but instead bounced off a corkboard panel filled to capacity with the thumb-tacked associate ID badges of newly-converted unassociate UAC members. G.E. scanned the IDs, relieved to find Trident's wasn't among them. However, Randall's was.

"The others," G.E. asked. "Supercenterintendent Benson, is he a prisoner, too?"

"Why the hell would anybody choose to live inside of a Buy-All?" Brett asked plainly.

"Not the G.M. too!"

"Everyone." Brett leaned forward. He pointed a finger at G.E. and let it twirl. "Including," Brett stood up, whistled as he sailed his finger into G.E.'s chest. "You."

"That's...impossible...." G.E. stammered, his face flushed. Memories of his dreams rolled over like a wave, buoying him on a sea of murky images, unfathomable depths, tentacles of corkscrewing air ducts, winding into infinity.

*Crack.* The sound of Brett popping a can of tangerine soda snapped G.E. from his fugue. He opened a second can and handed it to G.E. "We are prisoners, but what are you gonna do?" He offered a toast.

"Wait," G.E. said, failing to return the toast. "They say one person left. This guy, they called him Saul. They say he left a long time ago. I remember him when I was very young. At least I think I do."

"Where did you hear that name?"

"On voice chat. The Siege Arena. Some kid from #1364 heard about him."

"What did he say?"

"Only that there was only one person to leave. And he left this Supercenter. But the chat was cut. Management is always monitoring the feed. They cited him for illicit chat."

"Well, okay, there was once a person who left," Brett explained. "His name was Saul Zhener. He was..." Brett trailed off for a moment. "A kind man. A good friend. He was this old rabbi from Salem."

"What's a rabbi?"

"I know, right?" Brett suddenly laughed. "I'm sure that's what everyone else in Salem was asking." He rubbed his eyes.

Then looking at G.E., Brett could see this wasn't a joke. "Fair enough. A rabbi is a kind of spiritual leader, for Jewish people. He didn't get along with management. But we were close." Brett lifted the peace symbol that hung around his neck and revealed the opposite side—a six pointed star.

"Why not?"

"Several reasons. The final straw was your favorite Supercenterintendent. Benson asked him to partner with Father Trinity and form a Faith Department. Old Saul had this funny New York accent, too. I remember his exact words." Brett cleared his throat and affected a thick, Yiddish accent. "'You may not have noticed, but the Jews. The Christians. These are not the same thing,' old Saul had said. Then Benson gave him this sarcastic look and told him, 'It's not like we're asking you to worship Osiris. We're only asking you to go one God farther. Like the Jews for Jesus.'"

"If they are Jews for Jesus, doesn't that make them Christians?"

"Exactly. As you can imagine, this really set him off. Last thing he did was go around painting little red blotches on all the shelf posts beneath the compartments of the Jewish children. Next day he was gone."

"Nestlé and I have that red mark on our compartment!"

"Then welcome to the Tribe, kid."

"Thanks, but if he could get out, then we can too," G.E. added.

"We don't even know if he *did* get out, technically speaking," Brett countered. "Nobody knows where he is, only that he got out."

"Well, how do *we* get out?" G.E. asked. "There has to be

a way."

"Fine. You asked what a basement was," Brett said with a long sigh.

"From the map, I remember."

"Well, there has to be some sort of door that leads to it. And unless it's on the other side of the Shuttle Bay door, or in the security office, then it must be on the floor of the Supercenter. I've exhausted all my resources, and I can't find it."

"I've searched every inch of the Supercenter," G.E. confessed. "There is no other door."

"Well, keep searching. Here, some TV will cheer you up." He turned on a nearby plasma screen television, not quite as large as the ones that occupied the Electronics Department, but impressive nonetheless. G.E. slowly resigned himself to the tournament. One way or another, he had to ensure victory.

The Buy-Net was no place to find propaganda supporting revolution, unionization, illicit drug manufacturing instructions, or anything of the like. The network was heavily monitored and censored by a team of network administrators tasked with maintaining a healthy recreational entertainment environment for all associates. Unencumbered by the free exchange of information on the internet prior to the Closure, the Buy-Net represented marketing at its zenith. One could peruse new product information, customer reviews, notice of promotions, and profiles of exemplary associates.

News reports recorded from the planet Pepsicon updated associates on the Army's tireless war with the Schwags. These updates consisted entirely of good news, of course. Buy-All had learned that in order to be effective, journalism must carefully temper caution and be a stern reminder that all associates maintain a steadfast resolve. Associates were encouraged to unify in their support of the troops, for the sake of the entire war effort's primary objective—the struggle to bring Freedom and Democracy to these troubled, backwards people, the Schwags that inhabited the planet Pepsicon. Indeed, the News Division was staffed by the most talented marketers of all.

G.E. reluctantly sat down beside Brett and together they watched one of the popular situational comedies based on the lives of privileged Siege Arena recruits living on Center Aisle in a fictitious Supercenter. Aptly titled *Earning Our Stripes,* this sitcom featured a team of young Virtual Training Corps recruits sparring insults and boasting of their gaming skills amongst one another. Today's episode was one G.E. had seen before. The show's most notorious braggart, a short, curly-haired recruit named Twinkie hatches an ill-fated plan to gain an edge in the Siege Arena. Some bizarre ritual that involves wrapping his associate vest about his head in a turban and meditating comically while sitar music plays in the background. Twinkie challenges the show's good looking, humble, magnanimous, and impeccably skilled protagonist, Dole, to a showdown. Twinkie, of course, fails miserably in his attempts to short-cut hard work and perseverance. But, in the end, Dole sacrifices his own chances of winning to go back and defend Twinkie in battle, leaving the show with a sentimental, altruistic message, certain to warm the hearts of the viewing audience.

They watched together for a few minutes, until a commercial advertisement interrupted the show.

"This one is my favorite!" Brett said, perking up. The advertisement included nothing more than a white background and a pastel multi-colored array of All-Pods spinning around in circles, accompanied by the sound of electronic bleeps and bloops. After showing the All-Pods spin for a good twenty seconds, the video ended with a close up image of a human fetus, alone and adrift in space, wearing the iconic All-Pod earbuds.

"Bravo!" Brett clapped, laughing a bit too enthusiastically, the last vial of Tile Melt evidently kicking in.

"It doesn't even tell us what the thing does!" G.E. complained. Not an All-Pod owner himself, his words were tinged with just a bit of longing. A recognition of this longing within himself irritated him terribly.

"The All-Pod is the best-selling consumer electronics device in history. Notice the sleek, rounded design, the brushed metal finish, and clear, shiny buttons." Brett beamed. "You just want to pop it in your mouth, don't you?"

"And that's supposed to sell the thing?"

"Advertising is a lot like pinball," Brett explained. "Sometimes you only get that one shot. But if you make that shot count—one shot right in the *Amygdala*. The center of your brain, where emotional response and impulse satisfaction resides. That's all you need to win."

"Who cares about shiny buttons?" G.E. countered.

"Dopamine, my fellow inmate. Dopamine. The greatest weapon in the arsenal of the advertiser. Dopamine is the yummy chemical rush in your brain that occurs when you fulfill desire. When you see the All-Pod, your brain fires a jolt of dopamine, just a teaser, letting you know on a subconscious level that when you finally get to hold that shiny, brand-new All-Pod in your paws.... Well, that's when you'll really get to feel the rush. In the past, this was done with sexy supermodels. But that required the viewer's brain make an extension from the model, from the desire to have sex with the model, to the product. If the brain could not be completely convinced that acquisition of the product would in fact lead to sex with the supermodel, well, too bad, but then the advertisement fails. Personally, I miss the supermodels, but that's just me."

"So the point here is just to hold the thing in your hands?"

"Just to hold it in your grubby little hands," Brett sang. "That's right. That's all it takes. Nobody buys an All-Pod to simply have it, but to fulfill *wanting* it. To satisfy the craving of desire. Tearing open that box? Peeling back that plastic film from the screen? That's the foreplay."

"That's terrible."

G.E. reluctantly understood Brett was right, that this made perfect sense. He did savor the moment he opened the packaging of a new electronics toy. Realizing this suddenly made him feel uncomfortable, like someone had taken advantage of him. G.E. thought to himself that if all his hopes, dreams, and desires were the result of subconscious marketing techniques, then how much of who he truly was, as an individual, was of his own making? His thoughts drifted away from the television, from the confines of Aisle 39 entirely, and he felt very small and alone for a brief moment, troubled by the notion he may in fact be little more than a collection of manufactured needs and desires. The incessant drumbeat of marketing permeated his entire universe, and it became clear this was inescapable. He found himself at once drowning in its presence.

"I have to get out of here..." he croaked. Had he spent another moment trapped beneath its crumpled tarp, he may have fallen into a fit of hyperventilation. Or maybe the stale recirculated air prevented it. That the G.M. himself was an unwilling participant in some greater scheme, trapped within this *prison*—the mere thought of it dizzied him with vertigo. He stumbled from the murky aisle and back to the only place he could find refuge and comfort—his home compartment on Aisle 17.

That night G.E. dreamt again of the Merchandise Machine, but, this time, the dream became jumbled with his earliest memories of the Supercenter, when he lived with his parents, just after Nestlé was born. He didn't remember their home before Buy-All, but he did remember the day they moved in. It began with the sound of shattering glass off in the distance, a tepid panic, strained voices, and even at his young age, he could sense the first wave of fear pour around him. A brief hush followed, as the shoppers listened, their heads turned to the front of the Supercenter. The music from the ceiling was especially discordant amid the carnage that followed, and to this day, should the tell-tale violins begin playing on the overhead sound system, G.E. will clamp his hands over his ears to avoid hearing even one full bar of Christopher Cross's *Sailing*.

When the first wave of New Dixie soldiers came across the Missouri border, they laid waste to any and all infrastructure in their path. After retreating back to Arkansas, they left behind ruins. Chaos and looting swept Southeastern Missouri. A single platoon of US Army reserve soldiers took to defending the largest and most defensible building in town—local Buy-All Supercenter #1501. Local residents blockaded the parking lot, demanding access to the products they took for granted the day before.

Were G.E. and his parents not already shopping for baby clothes for Nestlé, things may have turned out differently. A mob of residents, seeking only emergency supplies first assembled patiently but shortly devolved into a panicked riot. Pushing and shoving turned to fisticuffs in mad and desperate attempts to find food, water, shelter. Shopping carts were filled with burning debris and flung into the doors which shattered and fragmented. The mob kicked out the spider-webbed safety glass and poured into the Supercenter. Some sought only protection from the mob, but others brimmed with rage, bent only upon smashing everything in sight. Before Christopher Cross even finished his 1980 Grammy-winning song of the year, the Supercenter had been reduced to chaos.

With the protection of the army platoon, led by a young Corporal Hildebrand, a group of associates and stunned customers, including G.E. and his family, fled to the corner of the Supercenter, and hid within the Automotive Department. There, something unexpected and unprecedented in the long history of looting and rioting took place. A faction of associates united, grew spontaneously loyal, and turned upon the violent mob. Perhaps figuring this was all they had left, perhaps hoping for some modicum of salvation from Buy-All itself, they rose up against the rioters, fought them back with tennis rackets and pool cues, rakes and watering cans, tire irons, and car stereos, until at last they persevered.

The loyal associates on duty that day, united with loyal customers going about their routine shopping, together blockaded the broken and shattered doors beyond the burned-out vestibule and sealed them with concrete and two-by-fours, never to open them again. What they found when they at last broke open the office doors leading to the deepest sanctuary of the Management office, cowering within the drawer of an empty file cabinet, was a diminutive man standing only three feet high. What they discovered was the General Manager, Sam Torino himself, congenitally afflicted with Primordial Dwarfism, frightened and bewildered by the chaos surrounding him, clutching a single briefcase he could have easily fit inside. He'd filled the briefcase with cash, the sum total of all currency that would act as the reserve holdings that backed the credit economy of the world's first self-contained Buy-All Closed Supercenter.

G.E.'s family was one among several dozen who rejected compartmental housing and instead camped in tents near the scarred and boarded-up vestibule at the front of the Supercenter. When it became clear that Buy-All would not reopen the doors, the adults were left with one last chance to leave or remain. Nobody had any knowledge of what awaited them on the other side. Anyone who remained would be guaranteed employment as an associate. His parents, along with practically every other adult, chose to leave him and Nestlé to the protection of the military.

As a child, G.E. concerned himself with nothing beyond playing in the vast Supercenter *Superventure Playland*. The military had installed an elaborate system of tunnels, slides, cargo nets, and ball pits that occupied the dead space above the shelves and spanned nearly a quarter of the Supercenter. He and the other children would race through these tunnels morning, afternoon, and evening until they collapsed from exhaustion. For the first few years, the children spent each day poring over a king's ransom in toys and games. Everything their hearts desired.

G.E. dreamt of crawling through the tunnels, the roof of the Supercenter so close he could reach up and touch it. He found a secret passage, a simple sheet of plywood upon the wall, lifted it, and found a passage into the adjacent Shuttle Bay. But instead of the X-2 Deep Space Shuttle, the room was filled with giant, industrial machinery. Pistons rolled up and down, threatening to smash him, fueled by a tremendous fire-belching furnace. He struggled to turn back, but the passage behind had transformed into a fiery gauntlet. G.E. dodged between blasts of fire, only to finally fall through a hole in the cargo net. He clung to the ropes by his fingers, dangling above scorching flames. Just as his fingers slipped, he snapped awake.

# CHAPTER 7

➡ **The Seige Arena**

**Chess is a game known** for protracted contests. Matches that go on for hours, with beginning, middle, and end game strategies. Of the many ways to win a game of chess, there is but one *fastest* way to victory. For every permutation of possible and potential moves, the calculations of which have boggled the circuits of the most sophisticated computers in the world, the fastest way to victory requires only two moves to a checkmate. For the opponent, it is the tripping over their own shoelaces at the starting gun. It is the fumble in the end zone, the bean-ball with bases loaded, slicing the drive into the parking lot. The draining of the pinball right after the launch.

So, too, had G.E. determined the fastest possible route to victory within the Siege Arena. After all, the Siege Arena was more akin to a chessboard than to a pinball machine. Where a pinball machine is subject to the chaotic potential of raw physics, the Siege Arena was but a graphical overlay of rote, predictable zeros and ones—without the element of random chance.

On the day of the tournament, the Electronics Department brimmed with excitement. The Siege Arena kiosks had been rolled out into center aisle to make room for the other associates to stand as an audience around the large 72-inch plasma screen. Rows of plastic chairs were filled first by Siege Arena recruits, the front row that of this year's potential graduates. Behind them, the junior, sophomore, and freshmen class of Siege Arena recruits. One other television remained as a scoreboard, continually updating the tournament ranking in real time, across all recruitment-designated Supercenters.

Competitors were not simply awarded points based on win or lose, but damage, tactical evasion, and time until victory all played into a sophisticated algorithm measuring a recruit's final score. A score of at least 1800 out of 2400 was required in order to earn passage and wage tournament battle against the merciless Schwags that inhabited the planet Pepsicon.

More than two dozen associates stood behind the recruits. Much to G.E.'s surprise, Brett stood among them, his first visit to the Electronics Department since stepping down as manager. Oddly, Supercenterintendent Benson wasn't present and, in fact, had not been seen outside his own compartment for some time.

Brett arrived just as Trident finished his own battle, Helicopter Pilot being his subroutine of choice. Needless to say, Trident's virtual Apache helicopter was the last standing after a dizzying six-way every-man-for-himself death match. While he qualified for a one-on-one match, Trident declined, insisting instead on a greater challenge. He lifted his hands from the controls, folded them neatly behind his head, and the score flashed upon the screen.

TRIDENT [#1501]: 1927 [pass]

Trident stood, turned to the cheering crowd behind him, and pumped a single fist above him. He locked eyes with G.E., who stepped over to congratulate his friend on qualification.

"I never thought this would really happen," G.E. said.

"What?" asked Trident.

"We would really compete. We would really qualify. We would really leave the Supercenter."

Trident look surprised at this. "You'd better get packing then. That is," Trident jerked a thumb over his shoulder, "if you've got the chops to win."

Where there had once been a safety, the Light Rifle had a switch with three settings that represented three common weapons, each with its own functionality. G.E. showed this to Trident, the dial set on the "sidearm" position.

"Pistol?" Trident asked. "Not your classic sniping play?"

G.E. flashed his eyebrows, gave a mischievous grin.

"Oh great, what have you got planned now?"

The visage of Sergeant Hildebrand, his horizontal flat-top like an artificial horizon, appeared on the 72-inch plasma screen behind them, a live feed from Fort Leonard Wood military base. However, his location was disclosed as the Planet Pepsicon itself, and a portrait of its alien, crimson landscape was superimposed behind him. Lips pressed, the sergeant called the next match with sharp, forceful syllables. This was the one everybody had been waiting for.

"Ten-hup! Fifteen-oh-one G.E. Westinghouse vs. Twelve-eighty-three General Mills in two-vee-two infantry Field Combat. Minimum 500 score to advance to the next round. Exceptional performance with a score above 1800 clinches deployment qualification."

Beside Sergeant Hildebrand's face, the timer counted down from twelve. G.E. took his time stepping before the giant screen. He tilted his neck left, then right, rolled his shoulders, and then lifted his Light Rifle to the screen. Upon a platform, G.E.'s avatar pointed a Desert Eagle .50 caliber pistol. What G.E. had discovered, what the programmer of the Siege Arena himself had never bothered integrating into the Desert Eagle subroutine, was that this weapon had no bullet-trajectory-deviation inaccuracy built in. Seeing no player ever tested it at long range, this oversight remained undetected all this time. A green grid traced over a series of wavy black contours, each dotted with uniform rows of crystalline blue spires, a crude simulation—artificial foliage. Unseen in the distance was his opponent.

If G.E. could best this top-ranked combatant from Supercenter #1283, it would bump him to the top of the Sharpshooter Ring, grant passage to Pepsicon, and exempt him from the rest of the tournament.

G.E.'s choice of beginning the round with a close-combat, last-resort side-arm puzzled his audience. His avatar looked foolish, pointing this pistol into the empty distance. The arena was designed for close-quarter combat between the spires in the lower field. The object of this map was to sneak and hide around the obstacles, peeling off shots at your opponent as he did the same. G.E. aimed carefully. Sergeant Hildebrand's eyebrows furrowed.

In the Siege Arena, G.E. contended, there was but one *fastest* way to victory. Every other contingency trickled down from the first second.

He took a deep breath and let it out slowly and evenly.

The timer clicked zero. G.E. fired a single shot into the exact center of the screen. The speakers erupted with the explosion of the rifle. A second passed. Then, a voiceover taken from the classic first-person shooter *Quake III* barked from the speakers: "*Headshot!*" Numbers flashed on the screen.

```
G.E. WESTINGHOUSE [#1501]: 2389 [pass]
  GENERAL MILLS [#1283]: 2 [no pass]
          Shots Fired: 1
          Accuracy: 100%
          Time: 0:01.
```

By winning after only two-tenths of a second had elapsed, G.E. earned the highest score ever recorded on the system. One shot.

Conversely, a far away and legitimately talented recruit named General Mills earned the lowest score ever recorded at two points for managing to survive but two-tenths of a second. He would have a long road from here, regaining enough points to have any hope of advancing in the tournament. Trident led the crowd in an uproarious cheer. He rushed out and slapped G.E. on the back.

"Game over, man, game over! That's what I'm talking about!" Trident said once it was clear that the round had indeed ended. The screen showed a slow motion replay of G.E.'s avatar firing a single round, from the hip. The camera then traced the path of the bullet, all the way to the opposite side of the map, where G.E.'s opponent had time to take but one step, not even enough time to drop from the spawn platform to the playfield, before his head split into a series of fractured bits. Of the many choices of sidearm, only the Desert Eagle could deliver a lethal headshot against an opponent with full health.

G.E. turned to his friend and handed over his Light Rifle. Trident punched him on the shoulder. "Always has to be some kind of game with you," he said, trying to resist sharing a mischievous grin. G.E. looked into the crowd and made eye contact with Brett, who regarded him with a slight nod and then quickly stole away to Aisle 39.

On the screen, the face of Sergeant Hildebrand appeared. The Sergeant squinted.

"So you know the spawn point," he grumbled. "Big frickin' deal, I say."

G.E. turned halfway to face him.

"Kind of makes it feel like...like...oh what's the word for it? Pointless?" G.E. said as he turned away.

"Son, if you are looking for a way to wash yourself from this outfit, then you just took the stupidest shot in your life." The Sergeant nodded ominously. The crowd hushed at once. "Dismissed."

As the crowd parted to let him pass, a single, blond head emerged. She stared blankly at her older brother. The paint on her hands hadn't quite dried.

"Where is your gun, Gee?" she asked.

"I'm done now, Nes." She didn't seem to understand. "We get to spend a lot more time together now."

"Are we going to ride on the space shuttle?" She scratched her nose, leaving a black smudge at the tip.

"It's more than a ride, Nes. We are going to Pepsicon. Both of us."

She looked up at the ceiling. "We are leaving the Supercenter?"

"Yes. Yes we are."

"I..." She hesitated. "Do we have to go, Gee?"

G.E. knelt down, took her sticky hands in his. "I thought you loved space."

"I do..." she said tentatively.

"And unicorns."

"Yeah..." She gave into a smile.

"And bears."

She gasped. "Are there bears?"

"Tell you what," G.E. said. "The two of us are gonna sit down tonight and watch every recruitment video on the Buy Net. We'll do some scouting and find out what this place is all about, how's that sound?"

Nestlé smiled.

G.E. left the Electronics Department amid the uncertain congratulations of his peers and headed to the Apparel Department, removing his vest along the way. He took a number from a nervous fitting room attendant and stepped into the corresponding stall. Someone had stuck their gum to the sign over the mirror that read THIS ROOM MONITORED BY VIDEO SURVEILLANCE. While it made him uncomfortable to know he was being watched, he knew it was just somebody's job and they had no choice, so he did his best to remain discrete and not flip the bird to the mirror or anything like that.

Because when he was off duty, he was a customer, and G.E. tried his best to respect that role and make life easier for associates still on the clock. Besides, it was far better here than trying to change clothes under the cramped ceiling of his compartment. He changed out of his uniform and back into his casual clothes. As usual, he found a pair of discarded brass safety pins lying on the floor of the dressing room. He picked them up, fastened them to his vest with the others, and slipped it on. Perhaps for the first time, the vest felt heavy on his shoulders.

The dire words of Sergeant Hildebrand turned over and over in his mind. He skated down the outer aisle, toward the former Automotive Department. G.E. took in stride the congregation of associates all dancing together to their All-Pods. They swayed to a common rhythm, all at once lifted their hands above their heads, held them there for a few beats, and then dropped them down again. Their wrists were absolutely encumbered in bracelets made from candy necklaces doubled over, or filaments of brightly colored plastic. Still, others had apparently plundered the entire stock of Shelly Arkansas' Supercenter Superstar Accessorizer kits. The girls had their long hair bound up in rows of berets, beads, or wrapped in thick yarn, all of which lashed dangerously about as they twisted and contorted to the music.

G.E. stopped before the mob, sighed, tucked his skateboard under his arm, and pushed carefully through deep throngs of frenzied associates, wondering for a brief moment how they might be *that* into music that sounded to him like a cacophony of electronic synthesizers arbitrarily laid over a repetitive, thumping bass line. It only made him feel all the more alone. He decided against entering the forbidden aisle and instead slumped to the floor beside the cold, mauve cinderblock wall. He banged his fist upon it, but could hardly hear his own knocking. No sound, no reply came from beyond. He slumped to the floor and held his ear to the wall. Only the vibrating hum of the air circulation system could be heard. He thought of the empty void beyond Buy-All, this solitary grid of Supercenters alone and adrift in space, each Supercenter trapped in its tiny cell, sharing in common only the Merchandise Machine.

He would find out what awaited him. Only one adult knew. He picked himself off the floor. He skated his way to Center Aisle and beyond, to Aisle 1, the Managerial Residence Aisle, where Supercenterintendent Benson had withdrawn himself for the last week.

# CHAPTER 8

➲ Aisle 1

**G.E. knocked on the steel** beam beside Benson's deluxe compartment at the opposite end of the Supercenter from Aisle 39—Managers' Residence—Aisle 1. On the other side, a disheveled and unshaven Benson slid a large piece of particleboard away from the curtain and opened it to find his student on the other side. As the drumbeat spilled into his compartment, a brief vision crackled through his brain. Benson saw around him a dark forest. Smoke filled the air. He could see patches of orange fire all around him. The sound of the Supercenter drumbeat morphed into the whizzing noise of a small airplane passing overhead. Benson slapped his palms over his ears and the vision evaporated, and for a brief instant, G.E. did the same, fearing the first few notes of *Sailing* had issued above.

"G.E.?" he asked, shielding his eyes from the overhead light of the Supercenter. "Come in."

Having never seen the inside of his teacher's compartment, or any other compartment on Center Aisle, G.E. was impressed by its size, namely, its height. Though it only occupied about one hundred square feet, it was as well furnished as a studio apartment. Benson slid the particleboard back into place and silenced the drum beat outside.

"Did you compete in the tournament?" Benson asked weakly. The room was filled with a stale smell, brought on by Benson's attempt to soundproof his entire compartment.

"Sure did."

"And you won?"

"I..." he hesitated. "I won."

"Why do you look so guilty, then?"

Piecemeal bits of foam rubber and blankets lined the walls and stuffed the cracks. Empty bags of chips, canisters of cheese dip, and wadded paper covered every inch of a long card table. Discarded Styrofoam plates, napkins, and three piles of clothing had formed near his double bed—clean, dirty, and mostly clean. The bed itself was an item of furniture G.E. had never seen before.

"What is it like there? On Pepsicon?" G.E. asked.

"What? The planet?"

"You said you'd been there."

"I said I had witnessed the enemy, and it is not a tale I wish repeating. You will find out for yourself soon enough."

"What about that manager? Saul Zhener? Did he go to Pepsicon?"

A fraught expression overcame Benson upon hearing this name. "So there is still talk of Saul, then? I figured as much. You'd think a man filled with as many wild tales of ancient mythology would be eager to build his own from scratch, right here in the Supercenter. But no, he did not want to play nice with other superstitions. I do recall he tried taking you and the other Jew kids with him. This whole 'Let my people go' routine. But we had a contractual right to all associates, The Buy-All Youth Sponsorship Program. Your parents signed up with Buy-All in exchange for your protection."

"So he left. For Pepsicon?"

"He's gone. And your parents are gone. And very soon you will be gone from the Supercenter as well. This conversation is moot."

"Will Nestlé get to go?" G.E. asked at last.

"Go?"

"To Pepsicon. She should be able to go."

Benson noticed G.E. staring wide-eyed at his elevated air bed. As an avid historian and collector of historical artifacts, the quilt was patterned with a reproduction of the Confederate flag. Misunderstanding G.E.'s awe of his ostentation, he assumed his quilt offended the student.

"Gah!" Benson blurted and raced over to his bed.

In a fit of panic, he tore off the quilt, began stuffing it into a ball, and then slowly turned his head to find that in doing so he had revealed his official SS-issue Swastika bed sheets.

"Bah!" he shouted and flopped onto the bed, contorting his body in an attempt to obscure the twisted cross. G.E. watched this with clueless amusement, having no idea what these symbols represented. Benson finally rolled on his back, covered his face with his hands and looked as though he were about to cry.

"War is no place for a young girl her age. But rest assured, she won't be far." Again, Benson's eyes darted to the left, as they had when he struggled to dismiss the HVAC Schematic, as if something troubled his mind that, for a brief moment, he could not shake. "Besides, we may win this war yet. Provided all this specialized training pays off." G.E.'s mind reeled at this realization, but knew that Graduation Day would come sooner or later. It just took Benson saying so, directly, for him to finally come to terms with the fact that he would be leaving his sister for an unspecified period of time. G.E. took a deep breath and lifted his chin. He committed to becoming a soldier, he spent his entire life aware of the Schwagist threat. It was his duty to defend the Supercenter, a duty that even Nestlé understood as paramount to their survival, their very way of life.

G.E. continued to take stock of Benson's odd compartment. He waved his hand toward the ceiling, only to confirm its height.

"This place is nice," G.E. said, distracted from the original intent of his visit. "How come everybody can't have a place like this?"

"A sound, if naïve question," Benson said as he rubbed his forehead and sat up. "I'm sure Brett and his band of splitters would like you to believe that everyone is entitled to their fair share of equal treatment, equal accommodations, equal pay."

"Sounds perfectly reasonable to me," G.E. said.

"You are still young, so your idealism is excusable. But you will soon find that the livelihood of the Supercenter depends upon a strict adherence to routine. These people don't want freedom, they just want reassurance they're happy. Brett's incessant prattling about rights and rules has done nothing but erode their contentedness. They have everything they could desire. Food, shelter, a climate-controlled environment, and, my God, the video games. Do you have any idea how expensive that Siege Arena machine is?"

"My sponsorship pays for my Siege Arena lease. For the good of the war effort, they said."

"Blast the war!" Benson yelled. "The free market is being supplanted by free love, don't you see? Our war takes place before our very eyes! The Schwags are here, G.E. They have infiltrated our very store. Some sort of spontaneous manifestation, I suppose. Or it's possible some kind of information is stored in the molecules of this Tile Melt." Benson's mind raced with deeply buried memories of a traumatic encounter at a Bluegrass festival. "Oh no, you may think it's all dress up, just a fun costume party. That's what they said, that it was just a fad, that all trends wind up coming back and then going away again. But I knew better! I knew it was worse than that. And don't think that it's harmless, that they are all out to save the trees or the whales or the whales that live in trees. No, they don't care about any of that. Filthy sons of bitches."

"But, Pepsicon, the Schwags of Pepsicon? How is it possible?"

Benson collected himself. "Right. Sure. You want answers, then? Take a look." He led G.E. over to a darkened corner of his compartment. He turned on a desk lamp, rotated it upward to illuminate a wall of hand-drawn charts and graphs.

"You see here." He pointed to a black square filled with a dozen or so blue dots and three or four red dots. "It begins with these red dots. They possess some kind of a recessive gene, I think. These are the carriers of the 'schwag,' if you will. It will remain dormant, usually until adolescence. Then it begins. They lose interest in work, a sort of primordial resistance to law and order. Exposure to shopping, products, accumulating assets—this causes expression of the gene. Some embrace, others resist any and all forms of marketing, preferring to just make things up themselves, regardless of the quality or the purpose. They'd rather play Frisbee than the Siege Arena. They'd rather weld their own haphazard monstrosity of a bicycle than own a state-of-the-art production bike. They do it themselves. Everything themselves."

"And what's this?" G.E. pointed to a second black square, this one contained as many red dots as blue. Tiny arrows pointed outwards from the red.

"Yes, this is called Resonance. The inclination against merchandise infiltrates the minds of adjacent members of the population. It spreads, like a mind-virus, but not through organic means. It's subliminal. Others can't help going along with it." He turned the desk lamp's spotlight to illuminate a third box, this one nearly filled with red dots. "Within a matter of weeks it will be too late to undo the damage. By this stage, all members have unwound into archaic proto-humans. You can rid them of merchandise entirely, but it is too late. In the past, we would simply entice them with bigger prizes—a nice office job. A new population demographic. Like-minded patriots. A hefty student loan bill offered a nice kick in the pants. So long as they never had a chance of amortizing that debt." He wasn't watching G.E. glaze over with complete confusion and just kept rambling on. "That'll get them to cut their hair, take a bath, and start saving up for a convertible. But when they finally figured out it was all sham, that there weren't any jobs out there for them. Well, that's when they started turning to Schwagism."

"Wow," G.E. said, certain of only the main gist—that the Schwags were taking over. Somehow. He pointed to a fourth and final box, so filled with red dots that it had taken on a diffuse opacity of red. "And this?" G.E. asked. "What do you call this?"

"Bonnaroo," Benson replied weakly.

"What's Bonnaroo?" G.E. asked.

"Manchester. Tennessee. It began many years ago, in 2002. An uncontainable field of Schwagism metastasized into a music festival so powerful that not even Bob Dylan could escape its pull. It grew every year until it consumed the entire town. We lost a good Supercenter there, three-oh-eight." Benson hung his head in mourning.

"Dear God...." G.E. whispered. "How long do you think we've got?"

"Four, maybe five weeks. It's hard to say."

"We need to do something. We should tell the Sergeant. He's an expert on Schwags. He will know what to do."

Benson clicked the light off. He realized he had already shared too much with this recruit. No matter, if he had indeed qualified, he would be out of his hair soon enough.

"Now, I think it's time you get back to your training." Benson shuffled him back to the door of his compartment. The visions were coming on stronger, he could no longer resist them.

"But I'm graduating!"

"Right, right. Then go visit your pal, Brett, I don't care anymore."

With that, he pushed G.E. back outside his compartment. Cut off yet again.

When the particleboard door slid shut, Benson fell forward onto his SS-issued bed sheets, hoping to derive the Third Reich's power of industriousness, discipline, and technological mastery through sheer osmosis.

Benson's fixation on the dangers of Schwagism wasn't

0126 JASON RIZOS

incidental. Now his thoughts had turned to this once again. He squeezed his eyes as the memory he had struggled so hard to repress at last bubbled up from the deepest recesses of his subconscious.

His wariness of Schwagism began after an unfortunate encounter at a regional Bluegrass festival when he was just eighteen years old. A teetotaler himself, during the night of the concert an itinerant vagabond thought it both comical and spiritually necessary to spike a young Ph.D. scholar's cola with a substantial dose of liquid LSD.

The last words Benson heard that night came from this vagabond.

"You want a hit off this?" he asked Benson, offering a filthy water bong that Benson figured might contain diphtheria along with whatever intoxicant.

"No thanks, dude," Benson muttered, his best effort at a nonchalance.

"Haw!" the man replied. "Man, this ain't nothing but schwag, it won't hurt you none!"

This word, this word "schwag," stuck with him as he walked away, unaware the vagabond dosed him with LSD. The word schwag resonated in his mind and became part of something larger, ephemeral, a drug, yes, but more. A philosophy, an ethos, and a portal into an alternate, future universe.

Benson, of course, tasted nothing. But not long after finishing his beverage, he found himself unable to operate his limbs, preferring instead to stagger, if not lope around through the crowd assembled outdoors in a grassy field. In the distance, a six-piece acoustic troupe played. Among the many visions that came to him that night, none were so clear and long-lasting as his vision of what he had dubbed the "ascendency of Schwag." As the effects of the LSD took hold, Benson pressed through the revelry until he eventually reached the margins of the natural amphitheatre and the banks of a small creek. As he lay upon a gravelly sand bar, the stars glistening and undulating perilously close, his body affixed to the Earth by what felt like an entirely tenuous pull of gravity. The stars eventually licked down upon him. A bolt of concentrated cosmic knowledge all at once streamed in from outer space and collided with his brain.

At that moment, the young Edward Benson gazed into the future. In his vision, though it only lasted but a second, he saw the entire globe overrun with dirty, filthy Schwags. It was no longer just a fashion statement, as it had been in familiar instances of the past. His understanding of what defined *Schwag* was but a little fissure of what would one day be unleashed upon the entirety of civilization. This familiar crust-punk-hippie that dominated the bluegrass concert was but a mere prelude to a sinister phenomenon that was yet to come.

In his vision, Benson saw droves of listless Schwags—a confluence of hippie and crust punk culture catalyzed with raw, pervasive poverty, an evil concoction indeed. They wore tattered, filthy black pants, clothing absolutely shredded and threadbare denim, canvas, patched occasionally with black leather, bits of metal pins and rods holding the frayed material together. Silvery steel pins and rods dotted their bodies as well. Ears, eyebrows, noses, lips—everything pierceable was driven through with studs, ebony discs, and thick barbells. Their faces were invariably decorated with tribal tattoos of a Pacific Northwest flavor, hollow ovoids of black, dark green, and sometimes maroon. Their hair was invariably dread-locked or at least at some indeterminate stage of dreadlock-ing, bound with pasty beads carved of bone or antler.

They did not treat others altruistically as one would ex-pect from their common ancestor—the hippie. They were as vile, cutthroat brigands. What series of events had led to this future world, Benson could not determine, only that this was a very dark time for humanity, if not the final undoing of civilization altogether. Technology was absent—these people howled and danced in a pagan, archaic ecstasy. They beat upon primitive instruments. Fires burned and crude weapons were forged from the artifacts of a ruined past.

Benson witnessed the post-apocalyptic crust-punk-hippie hybrid, an archetype that dominated the globe, an amalgam of all cultures and races, but only the darkest aspects of those cultures and races. Their appearance, particularly their savaged clothing, wasn't a fashion statement, but a genuine result of their lifestyle, which was less like the metal-studded punk look of those that preceded them, and more stranded-on-a-desert-island-for-a-decade like. As if a Hollywood effects artist had evenly rolled them in a careful mixture of sand, ash, and dung.

And they covered the globe.

Since that time, this vision remained a dark prophecy. Benson devoted himself to the prevention of such a fate, and now, for the first time, saw indications of its fulfillment within his pristine Supercenter. He tried showing up at the Education Department, but could barely articulate a few ran-dom pronouncements before his thoughts turned muddled and incoherent. Thus, he spent his time isolated, conserving his mental integrity, compromised by delirium.

Under the dim lights of artificial night, a pallor fell upon him, accompanied by insomnia. He tried exploring the Supercenter. He tried facing his ultimate nightmare head-on, to lose himself among unassociates dancing in their reverie. Benson understood that unraveling the bizarre rituals, the seedy drum circles, the apoplectic dancing—all the vagaries of which the Schwags were composed, was the most difficult task one could undertake. And furthermore, should he manage to penetrate the dynamics by which they resonated their sloth to the other associates, Pandora's Box had nonetheless been opened. Closing it was hopeless.

Once the lights dimmed that night, Benson crept from his stale compartment and strolled to a deserted Electronics Department filled with empty chairs, dozens of plastic snack wrappers littering the floor. The distant corner of the Supercenter beckoned with the faint sound of empty laundry detergent tubs, repurposed as crude percussion instruments. Aisle 39, an odd development, but one well in the making, as those associates bored and restless were now prone to congregating around this aisle for reasons too primitive, too carnal, for Benson to ever fully understand. Nonetheless, he found himself pulled to its center.

When the unassociates saw him creeping near, hearts leapt to throats. But united in their common purpose, spoons and spatulas banging on tubs, they found confidence. They watched him step awkwardly into their domain. Some remained seated cross-legged. Those that danced did not see him at all—eyes closed and bodies bobbing around a psychic eddy, a whirlpool in an invisible, circular sea.

At last, one of them approached the Supercenterintendent.

This one not an unassociate at all, but former Siege Arena recruit Randall Cunningham, who had hours ago failed to qualify for passage to Pepsicon. Benson resisted the urge to reprimand him, to remind the young recruit he'd never matriculate if he insisted upon cavorting with deadbeats like these instead of honing his skills in the Electronics Department. No, Benson did not—could not—speak.

Self-consciousness and anxiety gripped him as the memory of that traumatic bluegrass festival seized his mind. Perhaps Randall saw this, and perhaps acting out of sympathy, or perhaps wishing to allay his teacher's apparent terror, Randall extended a hand, a warm smile. His open palm held human commiseration in the form of a tiny eyedropper bottle filled with a concentrated solution of hallucinogenic indole.

He examined the vial carefully. Bathed in the lurid glow of lava lamps and balled strings of blue Christmas lights, the whites of his eyes shone large and iridescent, matched by the yellow contents of the vial, equally bright and iridescent among the otherwise dark scene. The Supercenterintendent, the Manager of Education, the Closed Supercenter Transition Liaison, second only to the General Manager himself, Edward Benson took the Tile Melt like he were the proselytized communicant of some unhallowed and wicked ceremony. The harsh acerbic taste snapped him from his trance, causing him to gasp while spontaneously vocalizing something that sounded like "*blurgh*."

The chemical intoxicant opened syntactical cages that, like the four-walled palace he ruled, had narrowed his perspective of the universe. A dream-like cloud descended over him. Benson unpeeled the tweed coat from his body, folded it neatly over one arm, and found himself enveloped by a profound openness, which confounded his senses, causing him to stumble sideways and fall to the floor. The grid of tile flashed and scintillated, bent and smeared upward upon shelves.

Randall looked on as Benson struggled to his feet. The Supercenterintendent waved him away and the recruit simply shrugged, pressed the earbuds of his All-Pod back in and resumed his bumbling dance.

This idea appealed to Benson and, in the breast pocket of his coat, he found his own almond colored All-Pod player. Benson felt light and loose on his feet, like a marionette. His muscles weak, he found it difficult to sense the spatial orientation of his arms and legs. As a result of this loss of proprioception, he walked with a jagged, lumbering gait. He stumbled like a puppet strung with rubber bands as he untangled the earbud wires. He pressed the tiny white earbuds into his ears and pressed the play button.

The music at once pulled the puppet strings taut. The track, part of a swing-jazz collection, the Jonah Jones Quartet's song *Where is Your Heart?* from a favorite film of Benson's, *Moulin Rouge*, took hold of his body, pushing him onto a set of rails.

And there, under the dimmed light, in the corner of the Supercenter, as the walls turned a crisscrossing pattern of flashing pinwheels and black security orbs dripped from the ceiling like great sticky blobs of glistening ink, Benson replayed this song over and over as he danced until the artificial dawn.

# CHAPTER 9

 **Graduation**

**The US Army had very** little interest in the internal affairs of Supercenters, but they did on occasion send a representative to hold an obligatory ceremony before a batch of recruits boarded the X-2 Deep Space Shuttle, ostensibly bound for the Planet Pepsicon, many light years away on the far side of the Milky Way Galaxy. Thus, Sergeant Hildebrand theoretically traveled this great cosmic stretch to welcome this season's batch of top Siege Arena performers into the official ranks of the US Army. The ceremony included all 312 associates squeezed down Center Aisle, save Sam Torino, who would watch from the security cameras in his office. Blue vests would be turned in for olive drab and a medal pinned to each recruit proven dexterous and cunning enough to rise to the highest ranks, cultivate the highest shot-to-kill ratios, and execute the most aggressive battle tactics.

Sergeant Hildebrand was a stocky man, his crisp, severe uniform kept impeccably sharp, clean, and austere. Even in casual conversation it wasn't unusual to find him standing in the military poise of *parade rest,* feet shoulder-width apart, shoulders square, and hands clasped tightly behind his back. A lifetime of active duty coerced him to even sleep in the posture of a prone parade rest.

Without a doubt, Sergeant Hildebrand found Graduation Day to be his least favorite military function. This was on account of him receiving far less fanfare at the time of his own recruitment.

Upon signing the enlistment papers, he became Private Hildebrand, was promptly and without applause placed on a bus along with nearly two dozen other young men and women who had the misfortune of attending the same college as himself and doing so without scholarship or trust fund. The student loan association worked closely with the military to see that the repayment schedule all but necessitated enlistment in order to wipe out a staggering debt no vocation had any hope of amortizing. The recruiter simply made him an offer he could not refuse. This offer being the absolution of his staggering student loan debt and the guarantee of a home for his young wife and son.

After all, Hildebrand realized too late, in no way could it possibly cost a student $40,000 per year to earn an undergraduate degree. And the US Military would not *really* reimburse the college this same figure for the honor of shaving Private Hildebrand's head and sending him to war against New Dixie separatists. No, his college degree was mere bait used to sustain skyrocketing recruitment quotas as war raged between the surviving bastions of structured American capitalism—secured safely within closed Buy-All Supercenters—and the newly risen South. Not to mention a third faction, the great betrayers west of the Rockies, the Pacific Coast states who happily let the Midwest turn into a battleground and buffer between themselves as the rampaging Southerners. The western states withdrew all support and declared themselves a sovereign nation separate from the East. As far as Sergeant Hildebrand was concerned, even more despised than those who started the war in the first place was the newly formed hippie-nation of Cascadia.

Four hours after signing up, Private Hildebrand found himself humiliated and harangued by a drill sergeant who would go on to haunt his nightmares to this day. Unlike this afternoon of decorum, never at any moment was his situation billed as an "improvement" or an "accomplishment."

However, today's military was much friendlier than back then. Buy-All proved itself a reliable source of new recruits highly skilled in firearms and already well-desensitized to the violence and danger attendant to combat. Or at least that was the theory.

So it had come to pass that Sergeant Hildebrand would visit seventeen Buy-All Supercenters around the Fort Leonard Wood military base in southern Missouri and laud commendations upon those he personally considered overrated video game junkies in order to impress the rabble. More difficult for Hildebrand than even this, however, were the silly lies built to promote the war. Like any good soldier, Sergeant Hildebrand was a terrible liar, but he did his best to follow orders and to preserve the illusion interplanetary warfare held Buy-All intact.

The moment Sergeant Hildebrand burst through the Shuttle Bay Doors, to the shock and awe of the many shoppers and passersby, he focused his eyes down the outer aisle and toward the blighted Automotive Department, where he could trace the smell of evaporating fingernail polish remover. Upon hearing the steady clomp of combat boots on the tile floor and then at last seeing the form of Hildebrand bearing down upon them, the sentries standing guard outside Aisle 39 at once abandoned their post.

Hildebrand threw back the tarp and marched to the rear of the Aisle, only to find both Brett and his top-performing, record-breaking recruit trading off turns on *Battle for Pepsicon Pinball*.

"I see you've taken this hacker into your little hovel," Hildebrand announced, just as Brett managed to send the pinball up the far ramp, where it wound around and settled gently into a miniature rocket ship.

"I see you've decided to come back and visit me," Brett said as he launched a new ball.

Hildebrand picked up one of nearly two dozen empty bottles of fingernail polish remover, sniffed the neck and winced. "You maggots been giving each other pedicures?"

"Yeah," Brett stepped away and let the pinball drain. He raised his arms wide. "Thought I'd open a salon, you know."

Hildebrand had no clue to the process of Tile Melt's manufacture and this was something Brett wished remain secret.

"The two of you can primp and preen each other until hell freezes over as far as I care. I'm just here for my graduates."

G.E. perked up at this. "We're going to Pepsicon?"

"*My* graduates are. Ones that know how to play by the rules."

Brett stepped up. "If you've got a problem with me, don't take it out on the kid."

"Something," Hildebrand squinted accusatorily, "or *someone* had to have gotten into his head. I never taught him that shot. He operated in direct violation of Arena rules."

"I did not!" G.E. cried.

Hildebrand pressed his lips together and his jaw shifted. "You shot a live competitor at Store 1283 without a single chance to begin the round. Damn near cost that kid his own graduation."

"Improvisation," Brett countered. "A good soldier takes no risks, exploits every angle."

"He deceived his opponent. It's bad sportsmanship."

"Sportsmanship, honestly?" Brett asked sarcastically. "Is that how detached you are now? Have so many war games turned war itself into a game? *All* war is based on deception. What the hell do you think we are telling these kids in the first place?"

"You watch your tongue, civilian. You had your chance to run the system the way you like."

"I'm just asking you, let the boy go. His turn is up."

"Ha. He will find plenty of other *turns* waiting for him. Infinite rounds of floor polishing, for all I care." G.E. dropped his head in disbelief.

"If G.E. doesn't go, I have the means to turn this place upside down," Brett warned. "You asked me to deliver a first-person shooter based on the America's Army gaming engine. You got your system. So where's my ticket to Portland?"

Hildebrand smiled as he strode slowly to Brett's face.

"Upside down, you say?" Hildebrand began, nodding, smirk still plastered on his face. "I've got news for you. This place is a goddamn utopia. I'm down to seventeen other Supercenters in my territory, and some are nothing more than aisle after aisle of assembly lines for artillery. You want to see this place go that route, I'd be happy to run a chain link fence around the Electronics Department, and you'll just be glad to have your bowl of soup filled every day in exchange for however many shells you can crank out between sunup and sundown." Hildebrand's face was beet red. He finally took a breath. "Come to think of it, I don't remember this sort of insolence when we found you deserting for Kansas."

"I did not desert. I didn't have any choice—"

"No choice! Ha! You begged us to let you into the Supercenter Project. You think things have turned around out there? They haven't. You don't know what it's like, losing communication with a Supercenter. You go there expecting to find a dozen well-groomed recruits and instead you find a smoldering black crater, maybe a few badly burned survivors, no clue what hit them. Their home picked over, the goddamn moulding ripped off the shelves. The enemy washes through like a wave of rats and disappears. If you want to sew chaos in this Supercenter, have at it. I'm after one thing and one thing only—personnel." He glanced at G.E. "*Quality* personnel. And I'll take whatever means to achieve it."

"And me?" Brett asked.

"What about you?"

"Will *I* be graduating too?"

"You will stay and await further orders, civilian."

"You promised at least passage to Nevada. That was two summers ago. Assuming the clocks in this place are working, and I have my doubts. Feels more like six."

"In exchange for a flawless training system! Flawless! Not one where all you have to do is fire a single shot at the starting whistle and kill your opponent. Plus, that little exploit cost me a recruit on my quota."

"You can't be serious," Brett began, astounded that

Hildebrand would both disqualify G.E. and betray his promise, all based on the same stupid event. But Sergeant Hildebrand did not give him an opportunity to continue. He sniffed deeply and scowled at the acerbic scent that filled the aisle and walked away.

"Graduation begins at oh-one-hundred hours, so man up, soldier. I expect to find you in the front row. You will support your fellow recruits who had the wherewithal to play the game as it was intended to be played."

Minutes later, the crowd outside the Electronics Department stirred with surprise when they found G.E. sitting beside Randall and the others who did not qualify, apart from the graduation class during the enlistment ceremony.

Sam Torino remained in his office, following along to a copy of the speech he edited for Sergeant Hildebrand. The Sergeant stood beside Benson, upon a dais, positioned at the threshold of the Electronics Department. Associates filled the chairs and sofas lining the adjacent aisles in every direction. Benson spoke into a box microphone.

"My fellow associates," he began with overdrawn sincerity, "before we proceed with today's graduation ceremony, I have with me this week's Letter to the Associate." Audible groans floated from the crowd. He produced a folded sheet of notebook paper from his sport coat pocket and flicked it open.

"Indiscrete alliances that precipitate between factions of associates have sought to undermine the tranquility of our Supercenter." Benson lifted his eyes, noted his still indignant audience, cleared his throat, and ratcheted up his bravado. "Our ability to unite in an indefatigable dismissal of Schwagism is essential at this juncture. But the vicissitudes of both commerce and defense are but two pillars betwixt which we thrive, not the four walls surrounding our sovereign territory..." Benson trailed off, eyebrows knotted.

He was certain this had sounded a lot better when he had written it, at the height of his Tile Melt daze the previous night. Rather than continue, he drew to an abrupt close, skipping to the last paragraph.

"As we prepare to send these young cadets to the Planet Pepsicon to deliver the Schwags their due reprisal, I ask that you reflect on the sacrifices you and your fellow associates have made in order to honor this day. And with that, it is my honor to introduce to you the onerous Sergeant Hildebrand."

Benson handed the microphone to the Sergeant, who began reading Torino's script. "It is a great *honor* to appear before this Supercenter today to welcome these recruits into the noble ranks of Virtual Training Corps cadets. These seven fine young men have sworn to protect this Supercenter from all harm, to preserve and uphold the time-honored ideals of American Exceptionalism. With their commitment, the path ahead will no doubt be fraught with peril, with great challenges, but also with great reward. These are the values we hold dear. Commerce. Merchandise. Democracy. And to that I add a quality of customer service."

He extended a hand and a smile. The crowd clapped weakly. "To these ideals, I ask these men standing before you today to respect the lessons acquired as expert recruits, accomplished Siege Arena champions, and loyal Buy-All patrons. Teamwork, patience, and maintaining calm under fire. In order to rise to the challenges posed, we must all remain vigilant. The seeds of insurrection grow all around us, and only if we fail in our commitment to preserve our way of life, unperturbed by the danger this war brings, dedicated to pride and respect, will it tear us down."

Sergeant Hildebrand beamed as he pinned medals on the recruits. The associates applauded. But Sam Torino found himself disappointed. The sergeant had skipped over the lines he wrote about the anti-capitalist socialist occupiers of Aisle 39 and the inevitable pitfalls of organized labor.

Hildebrand stepped down the remainder of center aisle, where the steel double-doors waited. With the turn of Hildebrand's Shuttle Bay key, a heavy click echoed in the chamber beyond. The doors opened for the first time since the last graduation ceremony, over two years ago. The only associates allowed into the Shuttle Bay aside from the graduates were the Junior and Senior class recruits. Other associates leaned forward and stole quick glances of the X-2 Shuttle for only a moment before the heavy doors slammed shut.

What G.E. found beyond that door was a drafty space consisting of unfinished metal studs, a ceiling of crisscrossing steel support rods, the unfinished plenum of this hastily built addition, topped by interlocking sheets of corrugated steel. G.E. studied its margins. The only occupant of the large room was a large fiberglass rocket ship poised at a forty-five degree angle. The oblong rocket painted in metallic silver swelled in the middle like a cartoon cigar.

It would have been clear to anyone with even the slightest knowledge of rocketry that this was a mere prop, a toy. In fact, the rocket had originally been built by Walt Disney decades earlier as an amusement park attraction. But G.E. and the other recruits' knowledge of interstellar travel was bound to the cinematics of the Siege Arena. In which a carefully reconstructed digital image of this very rocket was rendered, blasting through the void of space at speeds so fast that the pattern of stars stretched into horizontal white lines.

Sergeant Hildebrand, that morning, wheeled a portable steel staircase to a hatch on the facing starboard side of the rocket ship. Had the recruits an opportunity to walk around to the other side, they would have found the covered exit corridor. It was through this corridor that they, as had so many Disney guests, exited after experiencing their virtual space flight. The Disney guests would move on to the next attraction, but these cadets would step outside into the parking lot behind the Supercenter and be congratulated for having survived the flight halfway across the Galaxy without interception by enemy spacecraft.

What child, when shown a shiny silver rocket with puffy red fins would not be smitten and simply determined to compete fiercely in the Siege Arena for an opportunity to step aboard? So sound was the psychology behind this tour of the Shuttle Bay. Perhaps this class of recruits performed so poorly because they'd lost sight of this whimsical prize.

Sergeant Hildebrand watched G.E. carefully, looking for the same signs of envy that beamed from the other unqualified recruits. G.E., with eyes wrinkled and thoughts furtive, instead traced the outline of the walls and ceiling. His nose drew in the faint aroma of fresh, outside air.

As the seven qualified cadets boarded one by one, Trident paused to speak with his friend. G.E. nodded sadly, considered an apology, but words would not come.

Trident laughed at his friend's beleaguered expression.

"Come on man, don't act like this is even goodbye. I know you'll be on the next ship out of here once you get another chance to compete. Sarge just wants to make a point about hacking, that's all."

"I didn't hack the system," G.E. said with a sigh. He wasn't interested in defending himself to Trident. And besides, what was done was done. "Look, maybe there is something wrong with me, but I just can't stand the idea of doing what I'm supposed to do just because I'm supposed to do it." G.E. scanned the ceiling, counting the fluorescent fixtures.

"You could have won without resorting to that headshot right out of the spawn point."

"I have to get out of this place," he said at last. "Not to Pepsicon. If I could just visit another Supercenter. Maybe I can find this Saul Zhener, maybe he'll be with my parents."

"You have no idea what's out there. If your parents are out there, I'm sure they'll come find you when they need to. Just stay focused on your competition. Sure, everybody gives you a hard time for playing such a conservative game, but you are as addicted as I am. You're a born soldier and you know it."

G.E. didn't have to consider this long. He knew it to be true.

"But what if I did find a way out of here?"

"What then? You going to crawl your way through the Merchandising Machine to the next Supercenter?"

"Something like that, maybe." Thoughts of the HVAC Schematics overwhelmed his senses. He could hardly ignore the ceiling above. At that moment, a fog machine hidden in the Shuttle's tail kicked on. A blast of cool, white smoke blanketed the concrete floor and speakers issued an accompanying whirr. G.E.'s attention broke from Trident and he nearly pushed his friend aside to catch a better look.

"Anywhere but here," Trident yelled over the sound of the rocket warming up. "You're never happy with what you've got, you know that? You know that no matter where you end up, you'll just be unhappy."

"That's not true."

"Yes it is, the one thing you can never run away from is yourself. It's not the Supercenter, Gee, it's your insistence on asking why. Why do we fight? Why is there war? Where does all this fit into the Universe? What are you going to do when you have those answers? What are you going to do next? You'll buck up and fight, just like the rest of us."

A weight fell upon G.E.'s chest. He considered that maybe Trident was right. He could not, after all, really explain why he was caught up in the justifications for the war on Pepsicon. The war pervaded everything he had ever known. It was the reason for every sacrifice management asked of the associates. The reason for every abbreviated pay raise, every overtime hour, every motivation for top Siege Arena performance. The associates quickly brushed aside any criticism of management for the sake of liberating the Pepsicans from their terrible ideology of Schwagism. Was he just being petty? As he stood in tangled silence, the fog machine doubled its efforts and filled the floor with a dreamy, opaque cloud. One by one, the cadets climbed aboard.

"Look, Gee," Trident said at last. "I'm sorry, I don't mean that. It's just frustrating is all. Look, I know, I really know, deep down, that you're going to change your mind. That you've got it in you. I just know that one day soon you'll get to play combat for real, on the Pepsicon Siege Arena, and that first shot you take with a real Light Rifle *will* count. I get tired of the noobs and the idiots out there, too, but you've got to see past that. So this isn't goodbye." Trident had to raise his voice even louder to overcome the modulating pitch of the rocket. "I'm going to go, alright? I'll see you soon, right?"

Before G.E. had a chance to respond, Trident turned and ran to the waiting space vessel. Without looking back, he stepped in. Flashing warning lights ushered the remaining recruits through the Shuttle Bay Door and back into the Supercenter where they and the rest of the Associates watched the launch on the televisions in the Electronics Department. The Sergeant eyed G.E. as he closed the metal door to the Shuttle Bay. A second pair of loudspeakers filled the shuttle bay with a deep rumble.

A number of associates offered G.E. their condolences. Onboard the shuttle, the cadets watched as the display screen presented the corrugated steel roof of the Shuttle Bay. The roof slowly split open and revealed a powdery vista of stars above.

For the recruits aboard, hydraulic rods and levers tilted and rocked the ship ever so slightly in order to give the impression of accelerating g-forces, enhancing the experience of space flight for the participants, carefully strapped in for safety.

As G.E. watched the X-2 Deep Space Shuttle blast through outer space and carry his friend light years away to the Planet Pepsicon, his thoughts of what a mistake he may have made were soon interrupted by realization this video sure looked a lot like the intro credits to *Earning Our Stripes*.

# CHAPTER 10

## Sales Decline

**In the following weeks, drum** circles and lackadaisical unassociates repurposed as ad-hoc merchandise vendors took over every aisle, including Center Aisle, spilling into its deluxe chairs and couches.

No longer a recruit, G.E. spent his time mastering pin-ball, obsessing over an entirely new sort of machine. Though he refused to come to terms with the title himself, he was indeed counted among the unassociated. And perhaps led by his example, increasing numbers of other associates also preferred Brett's free economy to working pointless and obligatory jobs for the Supercenter itself. They participated in a crude barter system to satisfy their primal need to shop and buy. They spread towels onto the floor of the aisles, on which they displayed half-used rolls of tape, brass safety pins, colorful little baubles, discarded packaging, and whatever else they saw fit for trade. They bartered, often simply for the sake of trading, of diversifying their own proud pool of trinkets and debris. An incessant beat issued from improvised percus-sive instruments—upturned trash cans, storage containers, anything that would provide sound. The far corner of the Supercenter came alive with a pulse that ebbed and swelled, but never ceased.

Buy-All Supercenter #1501 associates found themselves standing in long lines, carts full of merchandise, but few associates remained to ring them up. Only then was it clear the division of labor collapsed, once and for all. If an associate desired a set of novelty wind-up chattering teeth, he simply set an IOU, hastily scrawled onto a scrap of paper, under the idle associate badge-swiper at an unmanned cash register and brought it back to his compartment. The associates found these sorts of transactions a bit anticlimactic, as the shopping experience itself was crowned with this transactionary moment, the satisfying act of the swipe itself. Of course, there was also the problem of unchecked credit run amok. Because they made no effort to maintain a cumulative total of their transactions, the shelves were soon stripped bare as the IOUs piled up without anyone to process them.

As the Supercenter witnessed the spark of a brand new and unprecedented culture emanating from the Automotive Department, Benson nailed boards onto his compartment door. Sealed safely within, the sound of their improvised drum circles could still be heard inside, as well as from every quarter of the Supercenter.

The unassociates now had a unifying tribal aesthetic. They dyed their hair with powdered Buy-Aide drink mix and ran keychain rings through the septum of their noses. They couldn't pay for showers without their associate IDs, nor for laundry facilities. A lack thereof, not to mention spending their days sitting on the now-thoroughly-unpolished tiles, exponentially increased the blackness on their clothing. Unsavory odors and a general disregard of personal hygiene were assuaged with liberal application of Shelly Arkansas brand Jasmine & Patchouli air fresheners, cardboard tiles shaped like guitars, rubbed all over their bodies. They wore a cake of black filth as a badge of honor, as a measure of time since they joined Aisle 39 and the UAC.

Some insisted the acronym was never meant to denote the United Associates Cooperative, but the United Anarchists Cooperative, a political schism threatening to undermine everything the UAC sought to accomplish regarding associate rights and collective bargaining. Their original stated purpose, established by Brett personally, had transformed from a mission of emancipation, to one of complete refusal to participate in any economic system, both physically and, thanks to the power of Tile Melt, mentally. The place of their nihilistic occupation strayed from Aisle 39 to encompass any and all aisles of the Supercenter. They decorated themselves with copious amounts of ad-hoc jewelry—padlocks on chains, plastic six-pack soda can rings were worn as bracelets, even frayed bits of fabric were layered around all parts of their bodies, employed as scarves or bracelets, or perhaps a headband, out of which a coil of matted, unwashed red-and-yellow hair would splay like a torch. Most interestingly, however, was their unquenchable desire to never work, but to participate in ever-widening drum circles.

Benson couldn't bear the sound of their incessant beat. He understood well the task of convincing them Tile Melt was a blight upon their formerly idyllic world was a tough, if impossible, sell. There was a reason for sumptuary law—to keep these substances out of the hands of those who couldn't be trusted to use them responsibly. Like he did. Furthermore, the associates had a cornucopia of approved cognoceuticals to choose from, prescription stimulants such as *Attencizin*, free coffee in the break room, and the irresistible taurine-and-guarana enhanced energy drinks. Drugs meant to enhance one's ability to perform regular routine, rather than derail them.

The Supercenter may have gone on like this forever, if not for a surprise video conference call from Sergeant Hildebrand. An overhead page was issued by G.M. Torino at once. A delicate, somewhat robotic feminine voice sounded overhead.

"Supercenterintendent to the G.M. office." The voice was soothing, sedate.

"Supercenterintendent to the G.M. office," it repeated, and then, "Code 901." This meant immediately, without hesitation, as soon as possible.

Benson had only set foot outside his compartment to visit the nearby, now less-occupied washrooms. He walked down Center Aisle for the first time in ages, stunned by the elaborate mural that Nestlé Westinghouse had painted upon the walls above the Optical Department—opposite Center Aisle. The formerly beige cinder block wall was now coated in black latex paint and colorful streaks of white and yellow shooting stars, galaxies, and comets. It had taken her over a week to complete, but Benson hadn't ventured anywhere near Center Aisle to see the artwork take shape.

He hurried on to the G.M. office.

Upon arrival, he found Hildebrand's face on the large monitor as it descended from the ceiling above Torino's desk. Before the G.M. could confess the total breakdown of his authority, Hildebrand started in with his own urgent agenda.

"The situation is critical," the sergeant explained. "We are getting reports of merchandise convoys being overrun by brigands. If the enemy is getting so bold to take on our convoys head-first, then we can't guarantee supply lines."

Torino wrung his tiny hands as he listened. He loosened his tie and pulled at the collar of his shirt, resisting the urge to glance at the panel of security monitors on the wall behind him. The array of monitors revealed a black and white frenzy—drum circles and dancing in every sector of the Supercenter.

"Well," Torino replied, "we seem to have a problem with the associates and could use some assistance. It's really not a big problem, it's just this UAC business. They think they've got all the answers. Anyway, their leader, you remember our Electronics Manager?"

"Yes, yes. I remember. You've got bigger problems than that now, Torino. You were expected to groom fourteen recruits this term."

"What? Of course. And we did."

"I counted thirteen."

"G.E.?" Benson interrupted. "You can't possibly be serious. He was our top performer."

"He didn't matriculate."

"You prevented him!"

"I'm not here to argue technicalities with you. Due to declining Siege Arena performance," Hildebrand continued. "I have officially downgraded this Supercenter to Materiel Support. As of this notification, consider yourselves commissioned as a munitions Supercenter. In lieu of future graduation ceremony, you will find all the necessary components for assembling FIM-92A Stinger rockets, save the tracking chip that arms the device, with the next merchandise delivery. I strongly suggest you have them assembled when I return. You'll need to set aside a space in your Arts and Crafts Department for fabrication. Assign your top associates to this task."

"You don't understand," Torino said, his eyes stricken with terror. "They aren't working! They refuse to work! It's pandemonium! You have to order them for me!" Hildebrand looked at him with crass disdain.

"I've got my orders, now you have yours. We need a dozen assembled rockets leaving with each truck. I don't care if you have to assemble them yourself, just get it done."

"You intended this, didn't you!" Benson shouted. "We can't possibly meet those numbers!"

"Can't is a word we don't use in the Service, civilian. I'm afraid you have no choice."

And with that, the screen went black.

"I believe we have found a new position for our forlorn Siege Arena recruit," Benson said.

"How do you expect him to comply?"

"If he really cares that much about the Siege Arena, and if his loyalties truly lay with Buy-All, he will do so."

Over the course of these weeks, with the Supercenter rapidly in decline, G.E.'s thoughts were preoccupied by his brief voyage into the Shuttle Bay. He dreamt nightly of the Merchandise Machine. The dreams began with climbing a wobbling shelf ten times higher than any other. Looking down, he could see the entirety of the Supercenter below him, the associates like tiny specks among the grid of aisles. Upon reaching the top, he struggled to hold his balance (reflecting upon these dreams in his waking state, he often marveled at the richness of detail.) Above him, on the ceiling, he found a corrugated steel ceiling plate, and with all his strength he lifted it. He then pulled himself into the space above. He found a vast expanse, an abstract web of silver HVAC ducts, an endless height filled with long cylinders and crossbeams. Gazing upon the vast distance above filled him with urgency and anxiety. For reasons he couldn't explain, he climbed upward, his progress slow as he groped at steel beams. He could not plot his route, but instead found himself lost amid kaleidoscoping silver ducts.

After waking from this recurrent dream one night, G.E. climbed down from his compartment and skated the empty aisles of the Supercenter, most everyone else asleep behind closed curtains.

This was where Benson found him, aimlessly circling the outer perimeter. G.E. coasted to a stop before him.

"You may still have an opportunity to earn the respect of your Sergeant," Benson explained, atypically upbeat, ambling about after another of his late-night Tile-Melt-inspired dérivés. "If you are truly worthy of distinction as a soldier, then you'll instruct the other recruits to begin work on the new rocket launchers. They are waiting on the Merchandise Dock."

"What? New Light Rifles?"

"Something like that. But not for here, for Pepsicon. Just see to it they get assembled in time for the next Merchandise arrival."

"When do you expect them to find the time? In between skirmishes? I'm returning to Siege Arena, duty, right?"

"That will no longer be necessary. This Supercenter has been disconnected from the Siege Arena."

G.E. was flabbergasted. "But what about the war? What about training for competition on Pepsicon?"

"These are the Sergeant's orders. If you can convince any of those rabble-rousers in Automotive to build the weapons, then perhaps Buy-All will allow competition once more. Perhaps we can even find a way to allow you back into the competition. You may have had your way as the darling of management, but after that little stunt you pulled during the tournament, you are under my authority now!" He squeezed his fists. "If not yourself then think of your sister! Do you wish to compromise her livelihood as well as your own? Your recklessness is sheer immaturity and it's time you learn to behave as an adult now."

"But sir—" G.E. pleaded as he scrambled for an excuse.

"Provided those rocket launchers are ready and assembled when the new Merchandise appears, I'll see to it your associate account is restored."

G.E. was given a choice—to comply with management and perhaps restore the Siege Arena, the sole purpose of the Supercenter itself—or not. Benson was pressing the issue of his loyalty—to disobey this order would remove all doubt in the eyes of management and ally him squarely among the unassociated. Though he detested Benson, and though he lost faith in management, and though he would not join the others on Pepsicon—he would not abandon his Supercenter. Plus, having not much else to do, he decided for the time being to work on the FIM-92A rockets. So he spent his days in Electronics, carefully assembling the rockets as if they were no more than complicated Light Rifles, toys for use with the unknown gaming system on the distant planet Pepsicon. But for all his effort it was too much from any one associate to ever hope to accomplish alone.

When exhaustion at last overtook him at night, G.E. dreamt of the Merchandise Machine, crawling further and further into its depths before the sudden shock of some terrible threat woke him. As he grew better at remaining calm and sticking with the dream, he eventually reached a point where the dream went further than ever before. During one of these dreams, as he climbed higher, the network of tubes grew denser, and G.E. feared he would be unable to navigate the treacherous footholds. But he had seen this place before and he remained calm. He climbed single, vertical lengths of rebar, just as they had appeared in the strange blueprint. After squeezing through a narrow gap between two large conduits, he pulled himself on top and found himself situated on the playfield of a gigantic pinball machine. A thirty-foot polished steel ball rolled toward him. G.E. ran to the top of the playfield, which he then recognized as *Funhouse*. The ball chased him down the Trapdoor loop, where the Trapdoor opened and into it he fell. The underside of the playfield surface was filled with a light so brilliant it at once roused him from his sleep and left him panting in his compartment, shivering in a cold sweat.

"The pinball machines!" G.E. gasped.

He poked his head from the curtain and found the Supercenter dim, the morning shift not yet begun. He tried not to rouse Nestlé as he dressed and hurriedly lowered himself down the ladder of his compartment. He found his neighbor, Huck, slumped in his favorite lawn chair and snoring gently, having spent the entire night in his chair. G.E.

stepped quietly over to his sleeping neighbor, carefully pried apart his fingers, only to confirm that indeed, Huck had in his hand an empty vial of Tile Melt. Huck was an ex-recruit who failed to qualify two seasons ago. Now that he had no chance of qualifying for graduation to Pepsicon, management would soon ask him to move away from packing and office supplies to make room for a younger recruit.

G.E. hurried toward Aisle 39. Along the way, he noticed something amiss on Center Aisle. A sleepy ex-associate tended a display of colored paper-clip necklaces and bracelets spread out on a bolt of felt on the floor. Her head lolled on her shoulders, her eyes remained half open.

Because it was still early, the concession stand was without customers and without even an associate attendant. The Electronics Department, and the famed 72-inch plasma televisions, sat cold and black. The other Siege Arena consoles had yet to be returned and the chairs from the graduation ceremony were still scattered about. For a brief moment, he considered he was still dreaming, as there was not an associate to be found anywhere. The drumbeat—had ceased? Could this be possible? Indeed, nobody banged on their drum, nobody at all. He walked softly toward the boundary aisle when at last he heard the sound of heavy footfalls.

Randall walked with his arms folded tightly about his chest, his head down, and his feet stomping in great steps before him. He couldn't hear G.E. over the music playing in his earbuds. G.E. lightly grasped his shoulder and turned him around.

"Hey Randy, aren't you on duty? Have you worked on any of the new Siege Arena rocket controllers like I've been asking you?" G.E. asked. Despite his own best efforts, G.E. had only managed to assemble two of the rockets. Randall and the other recruits hadn't helped one bit. Randall looked up, his pupils dilated into solitary disks of black.

"G.E.?" he murmured, pulling earbuds from his ears. He shook his head, wavered, and then reached a nearby shelf for balance. G.E. grabbed hold of Randall's shoulder and righted him. "This *is* the Siege Arena," he said, waving his arms wide. "Always has been, we just never realized it." His expression turned to confusion as he considered what he had just said, and then to terror. G.E. released his shoulder and his terror was quickly assuaged by a display of bags of shiny chocolate gold coins. Something was amiss, G.E. could tell. And he was right to suspect Brett as the culprit. In an effort to accelerate the derailment of Supercenter productivity, he dramatically increased the concentration of Dextromethorphan in his Tile Melt recipe.

"Whoah!" Randall said as he reached for the candy.

G.E. understood that this could mean only one thing— the Supercenter was fast approaching a Bonaroo level of critical mass. He wasted no time. When he reached Aisle 39, there the sentries twirled their makeshift halberds in circles, both slowly and unsuccessfully. The curtain rod dropped, rattled against the tile floor. The sentry found this impeccably hilarious.

"Brett's done it." The sentry laughed as G.E. stormed forth. "He's says there's enough for everybody. It's the end of work!"

G.E. pushed aside the plastic tarp, found precariously stacked rubber storage containers, brimming over with tiny breath-drop vials, picked over and empty. A dancing associate

spun in slow circles, knocked into him, and deflected onward
without notice. G.E. pushed his way through a crowd of
them. Brett's game room remained unscathed but occupied
with associates in no condition for gaming, or much else for
that matter, yet entertained by their futile efforts to navigate
a pinball machine, air hockey, or foosball table. Above in his
living quarters, the bed sheet pulled aside, G.E. found Brett
sleeping, sprawled on an air mattress.

G.E. turned on a desk lamp.

"Ugh...." Brett winced at the light. As his eyes adjusted,
he saw a look of abject anger and disapproval on G.E.'s face.

"What has happened to them?"

"I kicked it up a notch."

"You what?" G.E. shouted.

"It's just children's cough medicine." Brett pinched the
bridge of his nose and rubbed his tired eyes. "Says ages six to
twelve right on the label."

"It says *two teaspoons.*"

Brett lowered himself slowly from the air mattress, picked
an empty Tile Melt vial from the ping pong table and shook it.
When at last he determined it was empty, he pitched it across
the aisle and into a small waste bin. He opened a mini-fridge
and instead helped himself to a can of *Siege Star* coffee-energy
drink. Brett shambled over to his lawn chair, took a giant swig
from the can and let out a long sigh.

"Two teaspoons, huh?" he said at last.

"Stop playing dumb. The Electronics Department is a
mess. Nobody bothered cleaning up from the ceremony.
Randy thinks he's living inside a video game. We aren't
spending any time building the rocket launchers Hildebrand

ordered. You've given that drug to all the associates. And I—"
G.E. didn't know how to describe his current mood. He reflected on Randall's earlier remark. "I think I may be living inside a pinball machine."

"I did not just give them a drug. I have given them a path out of this place. By the time Hildebrand gets word of this, he'll have no choice but to let us go."

"You still don't get it, do you? Do you even realize this was what Hildebrand wanted?" G.E. flipped through a number of documents in his backpack until he at last produced a copy of the Merchandise Manifest.

Brett examined the blackened-out document. "Who did this? Why is it all blacked out?"

"It always looks like this. At first I figured it was you, that, or Keith. But then I saw the manifest form immediately after the merchandise flash." G.E. sighed. "It has some merchandise marked out, but just for Pharm."

"It's the cough medicine they've marked out," Brett said as he flipped through the pages. "They are hiding the shipping details from Torino? Why?"

"Did you honestly think Buy-All would just chalk all this medicine you've been buying up to stuffy noses? They *wanted* you to do this. They wanted an excuse to turn us into a munitions center."

Brett slumped deeper into his chair. The document trembled in his hands. "They really are that evil, aren't they?" he whispered. "Of course. No wonder Hildebrand played dumb when he found the lab. He needed an excuse to go from recruitment to munitions. Goddamn it. I should have known. He doesn't need warriors. He only needs cannon fodder. The

Siege Arena training system must not be working out on his end. I figured I just had to act fast enough, before they dropped the hammer."

"Then why did you do this?"

"Hildebrand." Brett took another pull of his coffee beverage. "He promised me amnesty. He said when he came to pick up his recruits, he would take me with them. That was the deal. I provide the world's greatest combat simulator, he gets his little training regimen, and I'm granted amnesty in Cascadia. He came up with a way to keep me here so that I would build him a simulator....

"I've been stuck in this miserable place for ten years now. But I still remember the first days of the war. I was working for the University of Missouri, just one year out from my dissertation. You think this place is bad now, this Supercenter used to be a citadel. They cut huge slats out of the roof. You know those ugly black circles on the ceiling over the cash registers? You can still see where they welded the roof back in. They had ladders running down, and twenty feet out, a circle of sandbags running around the perimeter. That was when they brought me here. From what I can put together, they must have had a kind of riot when the Ozark Libertarian Front took control of the State Senate. The local police locked the Supercenter down. The only thing in town, I guess, worth protecting. They didn't have much time to think about it, and, well, this was the place they picked to defend when Dixie kicked up her heels for a second time.

"I don't even know who is winning any longer. The South has its capitol somewhere in Texas, and the word is they won't stop until they re-annex the rest of the Union. Since we

Midwesterners are the only ones who didn't turn their back on someone, the majority of the Ozark Libertarian Front came here from the other states to fight. Many people held a grudge against the South for starting it all. I thought I was safe at the University, but that was their first target. They figured if we'd done a better job selling patriotism to America's youth, we wouldn't be in this mess. I was just a computer programmer, what did I care? But no, my Ph.D. was stripped until I went through their little Civics Orientation program. So I split.

"They caught up with me halfway to Kansas. I had no idea what kind of a war zone I was driving through. Some cities, some counties, some frickin' *neighborhoods*, considered themselves sovereign nations. It was madness. One of these sovereign subdivisions took us captive. Me and a bunch of other professors. Thank God somebody back at the University found out that we had snuck away. They contacted the US military, who sent this black helicopter that hovered over the horizon, looked like an insect, and made no sound. They sniped each one of the Placid Oaks militiamen before they even knew what happened. The training they had, it was...uncanny. But I'm sure that's something you are already familiar with."

"Ah," G.E. said, being at least familiar with the helicopter part. He nodded in affirmation, unsure which parts of this story had taken place in a video game.

"I was so naïve. I honestly thought they were rescuing us for the sheer virtue of it all. But they needed a programmer. They had been collecting 3D modeling experts for years, well before the war even. They had gaming technology unheard of in the commercial market. So I helped them build the Siege Arena in exchange for amnesty."

G.E. walked over to the pinball machines. He recalled the vision from his dream alongside this notion that perhaps he really was living in a pinball machine. He hadn't noticed it before, but Funhouse was situated on a large sheet of plywood. He slid the heavy machine off of the board.

"Hey! Watch it!" Brett protested. "You can permanently damage the tilt sensor." He paused. "Actually, that could be a good thing. Let me help!" They pushed the machine away. Only then did Brett notice the plywood himself and it occurred to him—this was the only place he had failed to look for basement access.

Brett lifted the large plywood board. There, G.E. found something he never before thought possible—a physical hole cut into the tile floor itself. G.E. carefully waved an open palm into the empty pit of absolute blackness, blacker than the greasy black finger paints that mapped out the darkness of space on he and Nestlé's compartment wall. He had now officially reached farther than ever before in his known universe.

"All these years," Brett said. "And it was right under my nose the entire time."

# CHAPTER 11

➲ **Basement**

**G.E. cast his penlight into** the black space within the tile floor. A short metal ladder, fabricated from cut shelving, stabbed downward to a second Supercenter floor below, not more than five feet away.

"It's all yours," Brett said.

"You aren't coming?" G.E. asked.

Brett waved a hand. "I can't leave it like this. Somebody is liable to have a bad trip. I have to finish what I started. Just promise to bring me back one of those black All-Pod players I always wanted."

G.E. nodded solemnly.

"I want you to look after Nestlé if I don't come back."

"You got it."

"She likes cereal for breakfast. Fruit sheets for lunch. Well, sometimes. Cereal pretty much all of the time, really. And be sure to throw out one *Attencizin* every morning. She doesn't take it."

"I will, G.E."

"And one more thing. I don't want her running around with these zombies. Don't bring her near Aisle 39."

"I promise. I'll see to it she gets to and from school. I'm going to set things right. Go on, then. Figure out what's down there. Oh, and one more thing. If you're honestly lucky enough to run into Saul, tell him..." Brett trailed off in thought. "Tell him I'm sorry I wasn't brave enough to come with him."

Without any further encouragement, G.E. tossed his skateboard into the hole and hurried down. He stooped beneath the low ceiling, into the uneven, dusty, and wet ground. He didn't know what to make of this unfamiliar, lumpy brown substance and couldn't guess how deep it might go. Beside him the cinderblock wall remained, drawing out the corner of the Supercenter, just as it did above, but the penlight revealed nothing but darkness and empty space leading away from the wall. When he breathed deeply into the vast, abyssal darkness, the stale air caused him to cough.

As he reached a point somewhere beneath Center Aisle, objects in the distance finally came into sight. He could see the ground lined with boxes, and, as he grew closer, could see these were long wooden crates marked with black stenciled letters and numbers. They continued this way, row upon row of these crates, until at last he saw a series of numbers and letters that he did in fact recognize.

**5.56 MM**

**BALL M193**

**20 CARTRIDGES**

An ammunition crate, just like the ones he would collect to reload his Light Rifle within the Siege Arena. This one, however, did not vanish upon him touching it. He lifted the handle on the lid to find inside a familiar sight—tightly packed M4A2 rifle magazines. These, however, were lined with pointy brass cylinders—bullets—objects with no digital analogue within his video games. The magazine of his Light Rifle instead housed the laser targeting circuitry and gyroscopic tracking system.

The box beside it promised M4A2 rifles themselves. When G.E. opened it he found just that—a neatly packed collection of six rifles, mounted on a metal rack, not unlike the rack beside the Siege Arena console in the Electronics Department, perhaps only ten feet above his head.

A peek into other boxes revealed rockets, mortars, hand grenades, claymore mines, Kevlar vests, scopes with red lenses, and long, slender rifles of another kind.

Something—and he wasn't sure exactly what—compelled him to recover his lost Light Rifle, and to slide one of the magazines into the breech.

Brett, his head still wavering above this black space in the floor of his game room, heard the loud metallic snap of the breach closing.

The radio on G.E.'s belt buzzed, startling him. It had been so long since anyone bothered contacting him. So habitually did he throw this two-way radio on his belt each morning, he had almost forgotten it was there. He pressed the transmitter button but hesitated to speak. He released the button. A voice scratched through.

"Oh now, now, now. What mischief have we gotten ourselves into today?" Brett's voice came to him over the radio.

"Light Rifles," G.E. said. "Dozens of them. And other ones, too. Ones I haven't seen before."

"You should probably leave those alone," Brett said. He

didn't even know where to begin with an explanation. "Yeah, I probably wouldn't touch any of that."

The boxes and crates grew more numerous, until at last reaching a second staircase. A metal hatch led upwards to the Supercenter above. It's similarity to the one in his dream was uncanny. Without hesitation, and just as he had done so in his dream on countless occasions, G.E. dropped the handle and lifted the latch.

Darkness.

He slung the rifle over his shoulder and carried his skateboard up into a vast, empty space above. G.E. trained his flashlight on a metal staircase at the center, and then the X2 Shuttle itself.

He tucked the wheels of his skateboard into the front flap of his backpack, slung it and the rifle over his shoulder, and climbed the metal scaffolding of the walkway. G.E. stepped to the top and peered down the long corridor. At the end, he saw the door marked AIRLOCK! WARNING DO NOT OPEN!

"I see a door," G.E. whispered into the radio. "It says it is an airlock."

"You don't mean to go through those doors, now do you?" Brett asked. G.E. continued forward.

"I'm going through them. I want to see the Merchandise Machine."

"Don't be so certain of what you do and do not want."

"That is the place stuff is made, isn't it?"

"What stuff?"

"The merchandise. Everything. It's beyond this door."

"That's correct. Everything you've ever known, touched,

tasted, desired—all created in the space beyond those doors."

"I want to see, Brett."

"I guess they didn't spend enough time teaching you about explosive decompression."

"I don't care."

"Go, then, G.E. Have a blast. However, there is just one thing you should know about that new Light Rifle."

"What's that?"

"It…" Brett didn't know how to begin. "It….works *without* the Siege Arena, let's just say."

"Sure thing, Brett," G.E. said as he reached for the door.

"Wait!" Brett tried to interrupt him, but it was too late.

With a loud *kerchunk,* the door swung silently open. A puff of hot air filled the corridor and G.E. pulled his t-shirt over his mouth and nose. Somehow, his dreams prepared him for this. Just as Brett began to speak again, G.E. passed through the threshold and across a signal dampening field that protected the Supercenter from any possible enemy detection and silenced the radio completely.

The former Siege Arena recruit from Aisle 17 burned in the fierce light beyond, sucked in the tonic air, and stretched his arms into the sky as the heavy steel door swept closed.

# CHAPTER 12

➡ **Outlot B**

**As the Shuttle Ready Room** doors parted, G.E. was at once bathed in a light brighter than any he had seen before in his life. The metal ceiling and tile floor that bound his existence for as long as he could recall were replaced by an unfathomably high dome of azure above and a flat expanse of asphalt below.

The open sky dizzied him, unhinged gravity, drew vertigo, and as G.E. stepped onto the gritty parking lot that surrounded Buy-All Supercenter #1501, he kept his hands firmly anchored to the gritty cinderblock wall of the Supercenter. To his left, a mountain of black plastic garbage bags lay slumped against the walls, torn and weathered into strips of plastic that trembled in the breeze. Beyond that, snared cargo net and foam-padded steel pipes, but in its present condition he did not recognize it as the Supercenter *Playland* from his youth, the telltale contents of the ball pit long since carried away by wind and rain. Bordering the parking lot, stood galvanized steel guardrails. Before a sharp embankment, a sodden gully and trees beyond. Flooded by sunlight, his eyes squinted and blinked, gasping for the dimness and shelter they had known all his life.

G.E. paced slowly around the building in a daze. He felt his way along the outside of the Supercenter, the rough cinderblock wall his only anchor to the reality he'd known just seconds prior. He clawed his way along, nearly blinded, cautious to maintain contact with the building, fearing he'd drift away from the Supercenter forever should he let go. He carefully stepped around drain spouts until at last reaching the corner, gripped a concrete yellow pylon with both hands, and pivoted around to the front of the Supercenter. Strange red ciphers printed on the outside walls proclaimed WE SELL FOR LESS and FOOD CENTER.

Evidence of an earlier catastrophe remained. A freeze-frame of the night of the Closure. Beside the hollowed-out vestibule, where automatic doors once snapped open and shut, stood a pair of toppled soda machines, two fallen juggernauts, dusted with mildew and long since plundered of both coin and beverage. The outside world, the edifice of the Supercenter, left to the devices of those residents of the town of Licking that remained outside.

As he continued to inch his way along the wall, G.E. came upon a mechanical steel carousel horse, its carnival paint chipped but otherwise in remarkable shape after years of exposure and neglect.

The concrete sidewalk just before the entrance sported a giant black scar, the site of some ancient bonfire, where bits of charred blue palettes lay waterlogged and ruined. A forty-foot lamppost had fallen over and now leaned against the wall of the Supercenter. G.E. shimmied along the post, hand over hand, used the lampost as a tether to venture away from the wall. He experimented with releasing the lamppost a few times to test the safety of straying away from the building. Confident he was tethered to the ground, the same gravity existed as within the Supercenter proper, he used the rubber toe of his sneaker to draw a pattern into the ashen pavement.

He dragged his feet around this area of the parking lot a bit, drawing a giant smiley face in the ashen, broken glass and charred remains before taking notice of the former entrance to the Supercenter. Shopping carts identical to the ones G.E. pushed on a daily basis lay snarled within the front entryway vestibule, a savage, twisted heap, their shiny, steel cages turned a dull rusted brown.

Nowhere in sight was an adjacent Supercenter as G.E. had been told his entire life. Beyond a twisted, broken chain link fence in the distance stretched a river of broken pavement, the once famous national corridor—Route 66. But there had to be more. He had seen footage of other Buy-All, he had competed with so many other recruits.

The former outdoor Lawn and Garden Department sat stripped of its contents, the very wood from its shelves. All that remained were tall stands of barren scaffolding. At the time the parents of that first generation left the Supercenter, G.E.'s parents included, many placed photographs of their children left behind on the wall in a hopeful memorial, but all that remained was a single two-by-four nailed to the cinder block wall and the rusted wire of what was once a spruce wreath.

The catacombs of the Merchandising Machine were indeed vast, G.E. concluded. Rather than allow himself to become overwhelmed with its spaciousness, he resolved to find and explore the nearest neighboring Buy-All, despite having been clearly and profoundly mislead by the recruitment advertisements he had looked to for clues to an external universe beyond his own Supercenter. After completing a circuit around the Supercenter, he surmised his best route— a path through the tree line beyond the Shuttle Bay doors. Surely, he thought, it couldn't be far to another Supercenter from here.

The path had been a well-traveled route for associates prior to the Closure. All that foot traffic left the clay-rich soil heavily compacted and free of vegetation. If not the distinct corridor of dirt, then its margin of discarded cans, bottles, bags, and other litter pointed the way through the forest. G.E. stepped gingerly over the steel guardrail, climbed down a five foot retaining wall, traversed the marsh-like gully, and stepped cautiously into the woods. The soft earth felt uncertain beneath his feet. He walked through what he surmised was a warehouse for artificial house plants.

He walked with a sense of urgency, sheer adrenaline now overwhelming the dizzying vertigo seizing both body and mind. Each tree mesmerized and invited him to pause and drink in the richness of detail in its bark, the complex array of branches and leaves. The gaps between the trees formed a seemingly infinite maze in every direction.

The blinding white light of the sun sliced through the overhead canopy in places, whitening the trunks and searing the trail with color. He marveled at the sea of plant life that exploded in occasional bouquets of fall hues. Burgundy sweetgum leaves blended upwards to yellow and shimmered like a torch. Pin oak remained defiantly green, dry-brushed with crimson. The brightly colored foliage gave G.E. the impression these were not yet ready for display among the other silk plants on Aisle 24. Indeed their leaves were rough and brittle, entirely unlike the plants he had encountered within the Supercenter.

Not far down the trail, G.E. came across a discarded soda bottle in a pool of standing water and surmised this was how soda was manufactured, but after stepping close enough to smell the stagnant odor, he thought better of tasting it and moved on. He looked back, only to see his rectangular Supercenter had become a solitary edifice upon the horizon, obscured by trees. Having now traveled the equivalent distance of at least six Supercenters length, surely, G.E. thought, the next could not be much farther.

Only on the flat screen of the Siege Arena had G.E. formerly experienced rolling terrain. He soon found kicking his way through the leafy brown debris beside the trail profoundly entertaining, by virtue of the simple act of destruction.

After a few hours of this, the vertigo began to wear off. With the waning sun he could now see greater detail. Soon, G.E. wandered through the dark of night, a night far darker than any he experienced within the artificially-dimmed Supercenter. But, beneath the full moon, and with his eyes well attuned to relatively dim indoor conditions, he could see well enough to continue through the forest unabated. He pressed on, certain that around the next corner he would find four cinder block walls and a steel staircase mirroring the one he left behind.

But that Supercenter did not come. Hours passed until at last he came to a stream. He sat upon the gravelly bank. Soothed by the percolating sound and overcome with fatigue, he turned onto his side and fell asleep.

# CHAPTER 13

⮕ **Reconscription**

**That next morning, the stark,** austere exterior of the Supercenter was greeted by the muted ping of an approaching diesel truck. Sergeant Hildebrand arrived at dawn, a tan drill hat on his neatly shorn head. He came to perform the same routine he had a month prior, swapping the previous trailer with a fresh supply of merchandise, a seemingly magical process that delighted and awed the associates within. Upon securing the trailer to his rig, he pulled away from the dock. As the rig rolled over broken glass and bits of burned plastic welded to the parking lot, he noticed fresh markings on the asphalt. The familiar blackened concrete scar and slivers of broken blue palettes had been disturbed. Perhaps some raccoon had simply come to dig through the garbage again. But suspicion got the best of him. He pulled the brake, flung open the door, and climbed out of the cab.

Sergeant Hildebrand walked a circle around the charred area and looked askance at an apparent circle drawn in the debris. Once he had inverted his perspective, he recognized a pattern scratched into the surface—the trademark Buy-All smiley face. He slung his drill hat from his head and onto the pavement and let out a string of unintelligible curses as he made his way back to the rig. He shut off the engine, marched through the Shuttle Ready Room doors and into the Supercenter. On the Shuttle Exit stairwell, he bent down, picked up, and examined one single, tiny brass safety pin.

A pair of stunned associates gasped as Hildebrand burst through the Shuttle Bay doors. Lips pressed tightly together into a perfect horizontal line, the sergeant glared just as a hacky sack fell soberly upon the floor between them, wilted and shapeless and sad. Hildebrand grabbed each of them by their collars. The associates turned limp as kittens.

"*He escaped?*" he blurted. "You idiots managed to let a Siege Arena recruit slip away?"

"Huh?" one whispered.

"Buh?" The other rubbed his eyes in disbelief. They looked down at the hacky sack expectantly.

Hildebrand tossed them to the tiles and made a beeline for Torino's office, casting aside shuffling, Tile-Melt-inebriated associates along the way. He beat his clenched fist on the door. Benson answered, his expression turning at once to panic. Hildebrand scarcely made eye contact as he marched forward to the desk of the G.M. The diminutive Torino pressed his remote control, quickly shutting off the wall of security monitors behind him.

"What are you two hiding?" Hildebrand demanded.

"Nothing," Benson said, thinking fast. "Strategic development meeting."

"My strategic ass. Where is G.E. Westinghouse?"

"I'm afraid you'll have to take that up with our former Electronics Manager," Torino offered.

"Brett...." Hildebrand balled his hairy fists.

"Brett was the last to have seen him. That is, that was

the last we were to see of him. That is, until we saw him—" Benson swallowed hard. "On the Shuttle stairwell."

Torino lifted the remote control in his arms and kicked off from the edge of his desk, spinning his chair around to face the wall of monitors. He turned them back on for the Sergeant. The video was already queued up. G.E. could clearly be seen ambling through the shuttle bay doors.

"You." Hildebrand pointed a fat index finger at Benson. "You're the one in charge of my recruits. You'll be the one to find him." He handed the Supercenterintendent an unfamiliar black device with a tan LCD black-and-gray screen. Benson flipped it over in his hands and read the back. "Defense Advanced GPS Receiver."

"Uh...." he asked Hildebrand. "What's a defense advanced—"

"It's D-A-G-R, but we call it Daggar. It has twelve channel satellite tracking, dual frequency reception, Receiver Autonomous Integrity Monitoring, and even a goddamn personalized customer service telephone in case you have to call me for help."

Benson looked at him, dumbfounded. "You want me to go out there, and what? Just find him? Into the woods?"

At that same moment, fifteen miles away, the wayward associate in question woke beside the bank of a stream. A light fog covered the forest floor. He looked to his left, half expecting to find Nestlé sleeping beside him. He was a bit surprised to find that the forest remained, for the most part, identical to how it looked the previous day. What he took for hallucination somehow persisted. Now hungry, dirty, and cold, only the stark novelty had faded.

He sat up, brushed pebbles from his face, and tucked his arms into his t-shirt for warmth. He tried piecing together his memory of the past several hours. He had found a path to the basement. He had walked out the Shuttle Bay doors. Up from his mind came strange and impossible bits of flotsam, a journey through a vast maze of green, nothing like the HVAC blueprint had promised, a fantastic dream fast corroborated by the arboreal scene around him.

G.E. picked his skateboard from out of a pile of leaves and looked around for a toilet. He stepped out of the stream bank, looked around a bit, and eventually urinated into a hollowed out tree stump. Guilt immediately took hold and he tore a sheet from his composition book, wrote *out of service*, and placed it beside the stump. He looked through his backpack and only then recalled the previous night when he had stuffed his backpack with unusual artifacts. Pinecones, rocks, and a few smashed mushrooms. He zipped them away and dusted himself off. A proper restroom, climate controls, and a dimmer switch at once topped his list of priorities. But before long, concern over his circumstances was assuaged by furious note taking.

*Expected a complex network of conveyor belts, chains, pipes, levers. Current sector appears suited for beverage and silk plant production. Temperatures erratic. Has not been properly cleaned in some time.*

He rubbed his eyes, already strained by the morning sun. His radio provided dead air on every channel. As he poked with his pen at the mud caked on the bottom of his shoes, he heard the sound of footsteps. G.E. scrambled to the top of the bank. A single traveler approached from the direction in which he was headed.

"How may I help you!" he shouted.

A girl about his age appeared, dressed in combat fatigues and wearing a green baseball cap with the big, bold letters C-A-T printed on the front, which G.E. took for the girl's name. Coincidentally, this was accurate. She also carried a rifle, which, when she saw him, abruptly leapt to her shoulder.

"How may I help you?" G.E. repeated as he waved. "I'm from 1501."

"You just hold on right there," she said, tucking the butt of the gun under her arm as she approached. Naturally, G.E. took this as jest, tilted his head with a sheepish grin.

"You have no idea what a relief it is to see one of those." He reached for her rifle. She stepped back and pulled the trigger. The barrel flashed and let out a concussive boom that set his ears ringing. He didn't notice the tree trunk beside him splinter.

"Dang that's loud! They don't make that sound at my Supercenter. What's it got, speakers in it?" He tried to pluck the ringing from his ears with his fingers. "What Supercenter are you from?" The girl stepped backward as he approached. "Hey relax." He cupped one hand over his eyes to block the sun, lifted his name tag with the other. "Fifteen-oh-one. Name's G.E. You know, light bulbs? Speaking of which, you know how to adjust the lighting down here?"

"Okay, that's enough." She looked down the rifle's sight at him.

G.E. raised his hands. "Look, that only works in the Siege Arena. If you don't already know that, you've got bigger problems than I can help you with."

The girl picked his backpack up from the creek bank and stepped away again. Individually wrapped snacks were an unfamiliar sight and only added to her alarm. Beneath the backpack she found G.E.'s M4A2 rifle. Her heart raced, never in her life had she seen such a modern, sophisticated weapon, leagues beyond her own half-rusted M1 Garand. She slung it over her shoulder. To her surprise, G.E. did not seem to mind.

"What outfit you with?" she stammered, dumping out his bag without lowering her weapon.

"I told you twice. 1501." G.E. nonchalantly stepped up to his bag and retrieved his canteen.

"Never heard of them. Where is this Arena?" she asked, careful to keep her distance.

"It's where we practice, you know, for points."

"You are a soldier?"

"Well, I have to level with you, Cat, I used to be. But I got kicked out of the program." He smacked his lips, discovering a thirst. "They called it cheating, I guess." G.E. reluctantly filled his canteen in the creek. The water tasted better than any he had ever had in his life.

"Wow, that's good water!"

"How do you know my name?" she stammered. "I have never even seen you before." She poked again at his backpack with her rifle. A bag of Blueberry Yummy Bears fell out. "What is a Yummy Bear? Where'd you get these rations?"

"Aisle 12."

She had had enough. "This is a restricted area. I'm placing you under the custody of Cherry Glens. I have to take you back to camp." She pointed back the way she came with the Light Rifle. "Now move."

"What's a Cherry Glen?" he asked.

"It's a—a place where, you know? Cherry trees—it doesn't matter!" she yelled. She found G.E.'s nonchalance disturbing.

Her name was Katherine, but she earned the nickname Kat among the other Cherry Glens militants. She was the youngest among them, and ever since turning thirteen just two summers ago and becoming eligible for duty as a Cherry Glens Cobra, the Lieutenant only assigned her to patrolling the neutral territory between them and rival subdivisions. This task bored her completely, and she had strict orders never to engage the enemy, but report back immediately to base. And now, six months into that assignment, she had at last stumbled upon her first enemy and immediately failed to obey her only order. But this capture thrilled her, and she was certain upon returning with him she would at last earn the respect of her fellow Cobras.

G.E., on the other hand, considered the whole predicament a joke. He nonetheless obliged her, gathered his belongings, and for the next several hours the two marched through the inner depths of what G.E. believed to be the merchandizing machine, which was turning out to be far more elaborate than he had ever imagined, quite literally, in his wildest dreams. He beheld its vastness with breath-taking splendor, stopping along the way to collect its various trophies—a small dandelion, the occasional rock, at least one of each type of pinecone, and several eggshell-white *Aminita* mushrooms. Indeed, he felt, a machine grand enough to create every last object he had ever known would easily encompass such distances.

"This is pretty amazing," G.E. called out over his shoulder to Kat. She had to think about this for a moment.

"What's amazing?" She looked around the dense forest, but couldn't see what he was referring to.

"All this. These plants. Honestly, how could we need so many plants? And these big ones." He patted a nearby elm with his palm. "What do they do?"

"You mean trees? That's what's amazing to you? You must be new here." It began to dawn on Kat that this was no Walden Meadows insurgent. This could go either way. The Lieutenant could promote her to Patrol Leader for capturing a rogue combatant, or assign her to Kitchen duty for disobeying an order. She had to come up with an excuse for abandoning her post before they reached camp. She pressed him about his origins.

"What's this fifteen-oh-one? Is that some kind of address?"

"Of course. What? You're not assigned to a Supercenter?"

"A Supercenter? Haven't heard of one."

"Tell me you've heard of Buy-All?" G.E. asked.

"What's Buy-All?"

"It's who we work for. I mean, clearly you're not an unassociate. Hey, did you get to compete in the tournament?"

"Okay, stop," she said. G.E. turned to face her. "Here's what we are going to do. You are going to start telling me what the heck it is you are talking about. Start from the beginning. I don't want to end up bringing back some crazy person that makes me look like an idiot."

So G.E. explained everything to her, from his earliest memories, to his schooling in the Education Department, his acceptance into the Siege Arena training program at age ten, the discovery of the HVAC SCHEMATIC, and his participation in the tournament. Kat, unfortunately, had never seen a video game in her life. She tried to take G.E.'s story as fact, but with every additional bit of information, she could only draw closer to the conclusion that he was indeed crazy. Parts of his story paralleled that of the manic ravings of a Cherry Glens Resident, this old codger she would occasionally deliver supplies to. Far from corroborating his story, she began to think the both of them were deluded.

"I'll just tell the Lieutenant you were armed and dangerous. And probably crazy. Or a Federalist spy trying to trick me." She motioned for him to get marching again. "Thanks for nothing."

G.E. concentrated on mapping the terrain, cataloging his adventure, still certain they were just about to come upon another Supercenter. At no moment did he consider the possibility he could be lost, as this was a concept he couldn't fathom in the slightest.

"We're stopping here," his captor said at last, motioning with the barrel of her rifle down a narrow trail intersecting their path. G.E. shrugged his shoulders, and marched onward. In only a matter of a few short minutes, they arrived at the end of the trail, marked by a pile of broken trees and brush. She motioned for him to move forward into the brambles, and they did. She lifted a Sassafras tree branch, revealing that the trail did indeed continue rapidly down a rocky ledge. On the other side, G.E. could make out some kind of structure below.

He assumed he had at last reached the next Supercenter. But as they grew closer, it became clear to him this was no Supercenter. A long row of felled trees and brush created a snaking barrier around an old church. Unrecognizable flags draped upon the steeple. Smoldering campfires dotted the forest beyond. Two guards stood at a break in the brush wall. A small, solar-powered electric marquis alternated between a warning, *all weapons must be checked at gate,* and the outdoor temperature, 65° F. The guards stood with their arms folded.

"You supposed to be on recon, Kat," one said.

"Watch your mouth, Conrad, I've got a prisoner here!" She spat back at him. G.E. stopped.

"You never said I was a prisoner!" he said. The two guards burst into laughter.

"This is serious, you guys!" Kat said and pushed G.E. through. The church itself was covered in black mold and ivy, its walls swollen with rot.

"No more talking," she told him as they approached the burned-out chapel.

"Technically, I'm on duty right now, so I'm going to act like it," G.E. said. He retrieved his composition book and took furious notes.

"Ambitious words for a captured spy!"

"Once I find my way back, all this is going on my timesheet." He pointed his green pen at her, his eyes squinting in the sun.

As they walked past a series of canvas tents, one man made eye contact, tapping two fingers to his lips, hoping this stranger may have brought with him tobacco.

"Como?" he asked.

G.E. tapped two fingers to his lips in return. The man shrugged his shoulders and then frowned.

They passed rows of tents where women tended large skillets over campfires. In the skillets, they cooked broken bits of circuit board until the solder and other precious metals melted out and rolled to the edge of the pan. Then they poured the metal into empty coffee cans. Ribbons of thin, black smoke lifted from smoldering circuit boards and heaps of bubbly, fused plastic were carted off. Behind them, a group of teenagers gleefully smashed computer cases with sledge hammers and sorted the shattered debris within. Bigger scrap projects required a nearby acetylene torch.

"Enough with the blinking." She stopped by the cutting station, picked a pair of nearly opaque welding goggles and handed them to G.E. "Here."

"This is your answer to the light problem?" he asked as he fit the oversized goggles over his head, the lenses jutting out at angles like the eyes of an insect. They passed others dressed like his captor, in green fatigues, carrying rifles of differing shapes and sizes. Just as they reached the old church, the doors to the chapel burst open and a man dressed in desert camouflage greeted them.

His name was Lieutenant Demetri Petrus and he was the leader of the Cherry Glens Constitutional Brigade. He was significantly older than Sergeant Hildebrand, but a slick-bald head and a thick, sinewy neck made his exact age difficult to determine. Petrus took one look at G.E. and was at once certain that Kat had overestimated her prisoner. He took a long, slow sip of black coffee from a dented tin cup.

"He says he's been trained for combat," Kat said. Lt. Petrus looked over the thin, gangly prisoner. "And he had this rifle with him."

"Federalist Army, eh?" Petrus asked. He extended a handshake. G.E.'s hands were soft, his skin pale, his posture less

than ideal, and his exceptional hand-eye coordination unap-
parent. "I don't know where he got that gun, but this boy is
not a soldier," Petrus announced. Having then lost all interest,
he turned away and stepped back into the chapel.

Kat would not be so easily discouraged, however. She
led G.E. into the church where the Lieutenant held a rudi-
mentary base of operations in the sacristy. Colored light
poured in from stained glass windows. The room was filled
with weapons of every variety and little else. A handful of
soldiers cataloged munitions, cleaned weapons, and paid
little attention to G.E.'s entry. The Lieutenant hovered over a
table covered by a topographical map of the region. Colored
toothpicks were scattered across the map, at least a dozen different colors, each used to represent sympathetic and not-so-
sympathetic militias of all rival subdivisions within a 50–mile
radius. Petrus allowed G.E. to study the map without fear of
possible reprisal. He did not know what this stranger's inten-
tions were, nor what brought him into Cherry Glens territory.
Even though G.E.'s eyes were masked by comically-oversized
welding goggles, he could tell right away that this was the sort
of person who wore his emotions on his sleeve, and that emo-
tion was invariably *awestruck*. This told Petrus that G.E. was
either crazy or had lived a severely sheltered life.

After Petrus examined G.E. for a few more minutes, he
concluded he was not crazy, but most likely had grown up in
some hidden Mennonite community around the Arkansas
border. It was not so unusual a story. Perhaps he'd gotten into
some ergot infested grain. Or maybe he had been traumatized
after witnessing the destruction of his community by some
cruel militia. Raids of this sort were known to happen around

the region. The Mennonites stocked ample provisions worthy of plunder—grains, baking supplies, hand-tools, timber, and livestock. Not to mention they were complete pacifists and would just hand these things over if you asked. Only problem was, this one didn't dress the part. Plus, the skateboard was completely out of character.

"Why is he wearing those goggles?" Petrus asked.

"Photophobic, sir," Kat said.

"Photo *what?*"

Kat pulled the welding goggles from G.E.'s eyes. He blinked like an unearthed mole. She then released them and they snapped back neatly in place.

"What were you after when Kat found you?" Petrus asked, marveling at the green-glowing Tritium sights and carbon fiber stock of the M4A2 rifle.

"Keeps saying he's from 1501," Kat said.

"What's that?"

"It's my Supercenter," G.E. whispered, running his fingers along the map's grid lines, which recalled the blueprints he had found within the shelf support column. He was dismayed to find no indication of the Supercenter within its bounds.

"Buy All? You mean those department stores they used to call Supercenters? One thing I sure remember is that Buy-All never stocked assault rifles like the one you got." He began disassembling the rifle as best he could, but was soon befuddled by the technology. "This is a model we haven't seen before, unfired at that. Besides, nearest Buy-All around these parts is in Licking. Is that where you walked here from?"

"No sir. I mean, that is, I did not lick anything. Just tasted some water running along the floor is all." G.E.'s attention drifted to the vast arsenal of weapons lining the interior wall of the church.

"We've got a lot of folks with a lot of problems out here, kid. The Cherry Glens Brigade's number one priority, however, is the reacquisition of the neighborhood proper." He mashed his finger down on the map. "Eminent Domain has taken on a whole new meaning. It's every subdivision for itself. Washington only cares about defeating New Dixie, and if they cared that much about protecting their own, they would have picked New England as their battleground. No, there's a reason they want to contain the fighting to Southeast Missouri. Wear out the enemy here, so they don't even think of crossing the Potomac."

It was clear G.E. had no idea what he was talking about.

"Tell me, son, are you a member of a Mennonite or Amish community?" Petrus began carefully articulating his words, fearful that G.E. was suffering from some sort of trauma.

"I told you. Supercenter 1501. We desperately need help. The Supercenterintendent himself told me he fears Bonnaroo may be in store. I thought I might find this guy named Saul Zhener, you haven't heard of him, have you?"

Like Kat, Petrus too knew of Saul, and it troubled him to hear G.E. mention this name, so he ignored the request. "Supercenter? You keep using that word, but Buy-All has been out of business for quite some time, son. Did somebody ask you to go grocery shopping, maybe?"

"That's ridiculous," G.E. said, turning his attention to the map. "What are all these toothpicks for?"

"This is what threatens the future sanctity of this community. Our enemies."

"Enemies? You mean the Schwags are here? Does Sergeant Hildebrand know this?"

"What the hell is a Schwag?" Kat asked.

"Why do they call you G.E?" The Lieutenant possessed a sympathetic, if condescending tone.

"That's my name."

"What's it stand for?"

"General Electric, of course."

"So you were named after a company?"

"Sponsored. For marksmanship. Just like she was named after Caterpillar and you were named...what is your name, sir?"

"The hell you know about my name?" Kat shouted.

"Relax, Kat," Petrus said. "You can call me Lieutenant Petrus."

"No," Kat said, finding herself at last fed up with the cryptic nonsense that came from G.E.'s mouth. "I wasn't named after some bulldozer, if that's what he's trying to call me."

Petrus reached out, yanked the cap from Kat's head and stuffed it to her hands.

"Oh," she said, studying the hat as light blond hair drizzled down over her face. Petrus walked to the rifles arranged around the far baptismal font.

"Federalists consider this place an occupied territory. Have us under Martial Law. Seeing that we aren't willing to let Walden Meadows and Forest Glen have their way with our residents, that makes us hostile combatants. Federalists would squish us all like bugs, should they find us out here. That being the case, normally we'd hold a Federalist soldier for treason, but we don't have that convenience during a time of war." Petrus lifted G.E.'s rifle. "You say you were trained as a soldier?"

"Of course. Only just about every day of my life."

"That so?" Petrus removed the magazine from the M4A2 rifle and tossed the weapon to G.E. "Let's see what you can do with it."

Petrus led G.E. to the roof of the church. Around the front of the steeple stood a small bunker of sandbags. At one hundred yards, G.E. could just make out a series of orange clay pigeons mounted on fence posts amid the foliage. Petrus slipped a single round from the magazine and handed it to G.E., who studied it, slipped it into his pocket, and then aimed the rifle.

Kat sighed, jerked the rifle from his hands, and flashed an empty palm. G.E. dug in his pocket, retrieved the bullet, and laid it in her hand. She loaded the rifle and handed it back.

G.E. knelt to the floor and leveled the weapon on his shoulder. He rested the barrel on the bunker and slowed his breathing just as he had been trained. At the bottom of an exhale, he pulled the trigger slowly. It occurred to him this was his first shot taken since the tournament. The rifle let out a concussive bang, leapt from his hands, and fell to the floor of the bunker. G.E. sucked air, clutched his shoulder, and winced in pain.

"You said you've done this before," the Lieutenant said, now seriously considering Mennonite or Amish origins. He lifted a pair of field binoculars and saw that indeed G.E. had hit the first of five clay pigeons. He exchanged glances with Kat, who nodded with approval, hands clasped behind her back.

"Open sights," she said. "Not too bad at all. Or a lucky shot."

"Again," Petrus said. He pressed another round from the magazine and handed it to G.E., who loaded the breech himself.

Upon bracing himself for the kick of the rifle, the impact on his shoulder lessened and his aim remained true. The tiny orange disc in the distance shattered. Subsequently, the third, fourth, and fifth shots all hit their targets straight and true. Petrus was stunned by what he saw, and wasted no time.

"I hereby conscript you in the service of Cherry Glens and issue you the rank of Ensign. Congratulations."

"What? Just like that?" Kat protested. "Is he even old enough?"

G.E. carefully set the rifle on the floor while rubbing his shoulder.

"No really, she's right," he said. "I've been through this before. I don't want to be a soldier anymore." He could not understand why these rifles operated the way they did, nor why it was necessary they set off such a loud pop. Petrus walked slowly to the edge of the bunker and looked out into the forest. He dropped his hands on the sandbags and drummed his fingers.

"You know what the French would do with an English archer that matched your skill, upon capturing them in their territory?"

"What?"

The Lieutenant held up his index and middle fingers in a V.

"Chop off these two right here," he said. "Keep you from drawing a bowstring ever again, with any accuracy at least. You'd rather I just do this? Then send you on your merry way?"

"No." G.E. looked at Kat. She placed a stick of gum she

had recovered from his bag in her mouth and shrugged her shoulders.

"Of course, I'd have to take your whole hand. Probably both to be certain. We could go this way if you—"

"Fine, fine!" G.E. shouted. "I'll play." If this was what fate had in store for him, then he was ready to enlist again.

"Splendid. I knew you'd see it my way," Petrus said.

"But what about my home?"

"What is it?"

"My Supercenter?" G.E. asked. "I have to at least go back for Nestlé sometime soon."

"What? Like chocolate milk?"

"No. My sister."

"Your sister is named Nestlé." He said flatly, finding G.E. hopelessly inscrutable.

"Yes."

Petrus began with another question, but instead changed his train of thought. "Where did you say you found him, Kat?"

"All alone in the woods. About five clicks south of base."

"That's Fort Leonardwood territory," Petrus said. "That's not your patrol radius, Kat. What were you doing there?"

"Must've got lost." She shrugged her shoulders. Figures, she thought, the one thing I get busted for, and I don't have any excuse.

"We'll talk about that later. Federalists have that entire region locked down. Kat, you know anything about this Supercenter?"

"I've been through there," Kat explained. "A bunch of big empty buildings by the highway."

Petrus had little interest in the details of G.E.'s departure, or the nature of his prior life.

"This is a very dangerous territory," he said to G.E. "You are lucky you didn't have your head blown off by Walden Meadows. Bunch of thugs, they are. If you are that concerned about your former allies, then you will help us secure this woodland. You can accompany Kat for the second leg of her recon sweep. Kat, take him South. Forest Glen got into a firefight with some Federalists yesterday. See what happened down there. And you won't engage any Federalist troops if you spot one. Just look at this rifle, you don't want to see what happens when one of these start going off."

Petrus turned to the staircase, then paused. He pulled Kat aside and whispered into her ear, making sure G.E. couldn't overhear him. "And one more thing—you stay away from that Saul Zhener, that *Moses*. He's an old loon and you're only going to get him worked up, talking about Buy-All again."

"Yessir!" Kat said, her interest in doing just that now piqued. She gave a salute, and the Lieutenant gave her a suspicious if withering look before returning the salute and heading down the stairs.

"What are we doing reconnaissance for?" G.E. asked.

"Recon," Kat replied. "That's what we do." G.E.'s head sank. "Don't worry," she added sarcastically, pointing a thumb to the sky. "We've got God on our side."

G.E. looked up at the fifteen-foot granite cross that topped the steeple, glowing warm in the early morning sun.

# CHAPTER 14

 **Recon**

**After his mission briefing with** Petrus, G.E. joined a line of Cherry Glens refugees outside in the cool autumn air. He held a tray before a line of cooks and each spooned increasingly unfamiliar and strange food products onto his plate. Huevos Rancheros with chorizo, toast, fried plantains, and fresh cantaloupe. Having eaten mostly dried, sugar-enriched cereal grains all his life, the fleshy slices of melon were peculiar, a little bland, and he had a hard time keeping them in his mouth as he chewed. But he nonetheless enjoyed these bizarre foods. Seated at a long bench and surrounded by boisterous people speaking Spanish, he took the time to document the experience in his composition book.

*Inhabitants claim their food comes from animals. These are not the plush animals of the Supercenter, made of polyester and acrylic. A tag beneath the tray claims 'con carne,' whatever that means. Exceedingly flavorful, and upon tasting another dish called 'chorizo' I can safely conclude that this is in no way made from stuffed animals. Nor does it resemble other animal products I have encountered, such as Yummy Bears, animal crackers, or Cinnabear Crunch cereal. I presume the Merchandising Machine assembles foods like chorizo in the shape of pigs for convenient storage and transportation.*

G.E. felt much warmer in the long-sleeved camouflage jacket and pants provided by the Cherry Glens Brigade. His jacket was adorned with patches of various size and shape. Small stripes, stars, flags, and symbols were sewn into the breast and sleeves of the jacket. On the right shoulder, a small circular patch displayed a hissing cobra preparing to strike. These patches had no significance outside the Boy Scouts of America, from which they originated, and now were simply meant to lend a general impression of valor. Beneath his jacket, G.E. still sported his old blue Buy-All vest. The Cherry Glens Brigade decided to repurpose his M4A2 and issued him a sniper rifle—their only Remington 700—and with it an impressive zooming device called a scope. This allowed G.E. to shoot targets so far away he would have to look into the scope again just to find out if he had indeed hit his mark.

*Toss a ball into the air and you will not find the roof, dig a hole in the dirt and you will not find the floor. The vastness of the Merchandise Machine is apparently boundless. As are the resources. So boundless that garbage is simply tossed to the floor. If only the inhabitants here appreciated the sheer amount of effort that Buy-All had placed into its construction, perhaps they might treat it with more respect. If Pepsicon is in anyway as vast, if its inhabitants in any way as numerous and diverse, then I can only conclude the task of liberating each and every one of them from the treachery of Schwagism futile. Speaking of, the threat posed by the advancement of Schwagism is lost on the associates in the merchandising machine. They are completely oblivious of the war. Perhaps it is best they not be troubled. They lack access to quality merchandise and in no way enjoy the comforts of life Supercenter associates take for granted.*

At 10:00 a.m., a stranger arrived at the Cherry Glens Encampment wearing black—a trench coat, leather gloves, wide-brimmed hat, a scarf covering his mouth, and a pair of black aviator glasses. When Conrad saw the figure approaching the gate with a strange, haphazard gait, his hair stood on end as he raised his rifle in alarm. Fog rolled in from the distant tree line, exaggerating the spectral eeriness of this apparition. Conrad trembled as he carefully aimed his rifle. The figure stopped and stood motionless before the guard as puffs of breath seeped from his scarf and condensed in the cool morning air.

The stranger slowly pulled the scarf away from his mouth to reveal the face of one Edward Benson. As Conrad kept a trembling rifle pointed at his chest, Benson produced a black and white photograph of G.E. flashing thumbs up and held it before him.

"That's G.E," Conrad said, somewhat relieved. He lowered his weapon. "That's the kid that showed up yesterday." Conrad led him beyond the perfunctory checkpoint and to the doors of the squalid church where he introduced him to his commanding officer.

"Great. More guests. And who are you?" Petrus asked.

"Who do you think I am?" Benson replied coldly.

"What? Why would you ask me that? Is it supposed to be obvious or something?" Petrus was a bit intimidated by the unusual demeanor of the stranger. Like G.E., his skin was exceptionally pale and, when he removed his sunglasses, he too squinted his eyes in the light.

"Isn't it obvious?" Benson asked.

"No, not really." Petrus folded his arms. "Are you supposed to be Mennonite or something?"

Benson presented the photograph.

"You are asking about G.E?" Conrad asked. "I guess he ran away from home then?"

"You could say that."

"One strange kid," Petrus added. "Private Conrad, when was the last time you saw G.E?"

"Mess tent. But he left with Kat. Recon."

"Heh, heh. He's out on a mission." Petrus swallowed hard, now considering he had possibly outfitted a missing pacifist with a sniper rifle. "They headed west, if you want to try and catch them."

Benson produced the DAGR device from his pocket. He looked at Conrad, then back at Petrus, then squinted.

G.E. was at that moment scaling the barbed wire fence marking the boundary of the Cherry Glens encampment, formerly the Cherry Glens subdivision. Tall rows of abandoned, desiccated corn stood on the other side. As he walked through the cornfield, he scribbled away in his composition book.

Kat looked over his shoulder to find him drawing pictures of his breakfast, along with a cartoon portrait of a bear followed by two strips of bacon and a question mark. G.E. stopped occasionally to pick up a pinecone and place it neatly into his backpack.

"Why do you keep collecting those? What are you, some kind of witch doctor?" she asked at last. G.E. gestured to the wide forest around them.

"Once I get the point of sale ironed out, this will all be available for shopping."

"That so?"

"Well, sure. I think that may be your problem here, Kat.

You can't have a productive economy without the proper exchange of goods and services."

"What, you expect somebody to buy this crap? What are they supposed to do with a bunch of pinecones?"

G.E. was eager to explain. "Well, all sorts of things! You can put them in a jar and display them. Or you can just collect them. There has to be some point to all this. Maybe glue 'em to something. Just use your imagination, you know!"

Kat closed her eyes lightly. "You are the weirdest boy I have ever met." She sighed. "Now, do you want to meet this Saul character or what?"

"Seriously?" G.E. perked up. "Why didn't you say so already? And aren't we supposed to do this recon thing?"

"Yeah, well, it's on the way."

Remington slung over his shoulder, G.E. embarked with Kat upon an unmarked path that led them through the woods and into contested territory between two other adjacent subdivisions nearest Cherry Glens. The three neighborhoods shared this thousand-acre cornfield between them, and like Cherry Glens, each featured its own paramilitary forces. Like most of Southwest Missouri, the region was fractured into hundreds of tiny militias, at first purposed with protecting upper-class homes from wandering bandits, but now warring with one another. The civil war between the United States and New Dixie, a contest that had grown too big, too abstract, to involve them, except when on occasion, caught within its crossfire.

# CHAPTER 15

Exile

**Kat led G.E. through the** Cherry Glens subdivision proper. The streets were eerily silent, and G.E. asked where all the residents were. Kat assured him they were inside, just hiding out.

"Cobras do a good job keeping this place patrolled. But you never know when Walden Meadows is going to strike. That's why we're doing this quick. If we see any Cobras on patrol, we tell them we have orders to visit this Saul. I've heard about some crazy stuff out there, you never know what the Federalists are really up to. I just hope you're right and not crazy about all this."

At last they came to a house just like the others, the curtains drawn over the windows. Kat pushed a button beside the front door and a loud chime sounded from within. They waited for a moment. Kat cupped her hands around her eyes and pressed them on the window, attempting to peek through a narrow gap in the curtains.

"Oh, he's in there," she said and opened the unlocked door. The foyer was connected to a dimly lit dining room. G.E.'s eyes were at once drawn to the far wall. He lifted his welding goggles onto his forehead and approached a glass display case that housed a blue Buy-All Associate's vest identical to the one he wore under his Cobra fatigues. The associate's badge clipped to the vest spelled out SAUL in neat, sans-serif letters. The display case also contained a variety of buttons, pins, and medals. As G.E. knelt down to examine them, a voice came from the staircase.

"Well, if it isn't a new recruit!" A peculiar voice came from upstairs. What followed was an older man, dressed in black, with fair skin and a gaunt face covered in a gray beard. "I see Cherry Glens is expanding. That's good news!" He slowly made his way down the stairs and took a good look at G.E. "And if it isn't young Adam!" He threw his arms around G.E. and gave him a tight squeeze. "Look at you, grown up now! What? You must be thirteen! And I suspect not even mitzvahed!"

"Fifteen, and I'm G.E., sir. That is, my name is G.E."

"Yes," the man squinted. "I remember that as well." He appeared suddenly overwhelmed with anguish. "Tell me your sister is alright?"

"Nestlé? Of course. She's waiting for me right now in Aisle 17. I should probably get back before long."

"You don't remember me, do you, boy? That's understandable. Your parents will be quite pleased to see you are alright. But they didn't send you out here to fight us? Like the others?"

"No sir. I left on my own. Through the basement," G.E. explained.

"The basement! Marvelous!" Only then did he seem to recover and notice Kat. "And good morning to you, Katherine. And what brings you here?"

"Him." Arms folded, she pointed an elbow to G.E. "Wanted to make sure he wasn't crazy." She blushed as soon as she said this. "I don't mean to say that you are crazy, sir, I just didn't know anything about Supercenters, is all."

Saul smiled at this. "Yes, and they aim to keep it that way."

"Oh," said G.E. "Brett says he's sorry he couldn't be here." This turned G.E.'s attention back to his initial goal. "Mr. Zhener, you don't happen to know where I can find our parents?"

"Yes, yes. Of course. I keep strict records! Very strict!" Saul opened a drawer beneath the glass display case and from it lifted a hefty, leather-bound tome. He flipped through the pages, all hand-lettered, and ran his fingers down a list of names. "Let's see here...Levit. Yes. Your parents are currently residing in Supercenter #1503. Springfield." It took G.E. a moment to recognize this surname as his own, so long had it been since he last heard it.

"How far away is that?"

"Well, not too far." Saul stroked his beard as he considered this. "Used to be, that is."

"It's very far," Kat said flatly. "Springfield? That's like halfway across the state from here. You couldn't do it without a vehicle. And then you'd have at least a dozen militias to convince letting you pass. Impossible."

"Yes," Saul said at last. "She is probably right. And nobody has any transportation any longer. Except the military, of course." Saul lifted a black fedora hat and black trench coat from a pair of hooks beside the front door. "And speaking of long commutes. I'm late for a journey of my own."

Kat looked shocked. "I would advise against leaving the subdivision proper, sir. Do you even have the proper authorization from the Lieutenant?"

"Don't worry, young lady. I'll be safe."

"But what about Walden Meadows?" Kat asked.

"What interest do they have in an old man like me? Besides, there are some kids out there putting together a commune. It's really a kibbutz, they just don't know it yet."

G.E. looked defeated. "I've made it this far, I can make it farther. Just point me the way."

"Don't be dumb," Kat said. "You don't even understand distances. This is probably the farthest you've ever walked in your whole life." She could sense the look of desperation overcoming G.E. and softened her words. "Look, I'll help you, okay? I'll help you find it, but we have to get going now."

They stepped back into the street and, after a long hug for the both of them, parted ways with Saul Zhener. G.E. looked at the distant horizon, wondered how many more like it he would have to pass before reaching Buy-All Supercenter #1503.

And just beyond that rolling horizon, his former teacher, Edward Benson, circled a cornfield. DAGR navigator in hand, he was yet unable to point himself to G.E.'s location. The more he fiddled with the unit, the more it seemed to throw him off track. In a fit of frustration, he mashed the rubber keypad. The device asked if he would like to select a different primary language.

"Fine. Be like that," he whispered out loud. "Let the kid rot out here." He dialed the number to Sergeant Hildebrand and lifted the device to his ear.

"This better be good," Hildebrand answered.

"I've found him," Benson whispered, alone in the woods.

"Good. Bring him back."

"I don't think he's interested."

"What? Tell him this is an order," Hildebrand insisted.

"He's bargained his way into one of those militias. No doubt he's poisoned them against Buy-All."

"Please tell me you are joking. Does he know how to lead them back to the Supercenter?"

"I don't think so. Anybody who has spent as many years as him trapped in a Supercenter is bound it get lost. Besides, I've convinced them that he's crazy."

"Delusional?" Hildebrand asked.

"Pacifist."

"Better yet. Ping the location of the camp on your DAGR and I'll send in a drone to target the base for an air strike."

"My pleasure," Benson said, terminating the call. He zoomed out on the digital map and tried to pinpoint the location he just left. But he had little clue how to operate the device. He wasn't certain if the scale at the top of the screen was meant to represent the tiny black bar below it or the width of the entire screen. He did his best to estimate the location of the Cherry Glens encampment and forwarded the coordinates to Hildebrand.

"That should be right." He next made an equally specious calculation and headed off in a direction he presumed would lead him back to the Supercenter. For hours, Benson followed dried creek beds and traversed crumbling hilltops, zooming in and out on his puzzling navigation device. What looked like a junked car in the distance assured him he was at least nearby civilization, nearby enough that he would at least come across a road of some sort. The device was unable to account for changes in terrain, or obstacles such as sudden, unscalable cliffs, and merely pointed a direct line back to the Supercenter. He found himself pushing brush and debris aside as he slowly zig-zagged his way through the forest, only to check his navigator and find he had once more strayed from his route.

Benson figured the more time he spent with his eyes on the navigator, the less he spent tracking his way through the woods. He fixed his eyes on a place on the horizon, a gap in the trees, thinking this thinning up ahead was on account of the cornfield just beyond. Once he got back to the cornfield, he surmised, then surely he could re-orient himself and allow the DAGR to fix a better path than this. But when at last he reached the gap, he found only a slight downhill on the other side—and with it more trees. Rather than descend—a downhill would only lead to another insufferable uphill—he instead followed along the ridge, the general direction the DAGR suggested, until at last, the sun now high into the sky, he came across an old, rusted-out 1940-something Plymouth.

Meanwhile, Kat and G.E. had reached Highway 63. The highway cut alongside a steep ridge and provided a high vantage point over the continuing wilderness below.

The longest side of the cornfield ran adjacent to this nearly 1,300 mile corridor that divided the country in half from Wisconsin to Louisiana. Now well into an August drought, the field consisted of bone-white stalks of corn, dry and petrified, with thick patches of clover and dandelion growing up between them. Occasionally, the corn would vanish in places where it had burned earlier in the season, the soil already reclaimed by jimson weed and tall musk thistle. The two pushed quickly through the tall rows of dead corn but walked carefully through these pioneer meadows, scanning the horizon for enemies through the scope of G.E.'s Remington.

"This, I think this may be important," G.E. said, upon finally setting foot upon the highway. He kneeled on the pavement and patting the smooth roadway with his hands. "This material. A similar surface lies outside the Supercenter. I think this is *Outlot*. It was spread out all over the place at the Supercenter."

"That's really fascinating and all," Kat said. "But really, it's just a road."

"Some kind of an energy conduit...." G.E. whispered. "Yes! I've seen this in a training video! Beams of energy, some kind of electric pulse, or plasma energy, shoots down these conduits to each Supercenter." His expression turned suddenly grave. "Kat, I think this will lead us to the Supercenter!"

"I'm sure it will," Kat said, rolling her eyes. "It's a road." She bent down and patted the asphalt, pronouncing it slowly for him, "Row-Add."

A snapping branch sounded in the distant woods.

"What was that sound?" G.E. asked.

"What? That creaking sound? That's just the wind in the trees."

Down below the guardrail opposite the cornfield, G.E. spotted saw a single figure climbing through the underbrush. The person straddled a rusted barbwire fence and fell down on the other side. G.E. pointed his rifle down the hill. Peering through the scope to a distance of five hundred yards, he could make out that it was apparently unarmed, but wore a military uniform, one that resembled the uniform he knew from his Supercenter.

"Looks like my old uniform," he whispered to Kat.

"Federales," Kat whispered back.

At two hundred yards, still approaching, struggling through the broken rows of corn, G.E. could at last make out a face. He recognized his former teammate and ally, Trident. He sputtered with giddy excitement, covered his mouth and laughed into his palm.

"What's so funny?" Kat whispered. G.E. could not wait to see the look on his friend's face when he suddenly found himself counted out of a match he didn't know he was engaged in!

"Watch this!" he said. G.E. raised the rifle to his eye, focused on Trident's chest, stifled his laughter, and just as Kat shouted "DON'T" at the top of her lungs, pulled the trigger.

# CHAPTER 16

➲ **Debriefing**

**For all his practice and** precision, G.E. failed to hit Trident in the head, instead penetrating his shoulder below the collarbone and out the backside. Trident felt the bullet sting him, and then a half second later, the familiar report of the rifle.

The blood was unexpected. He hadn't been shot before, but was now plenty sure it had intended to kill him. He looked up at the sky and the first thing he thought was how nice it was to finally be off his feet. A moment later, the pain set in. And then the face of G.E. hovered above him first grinning and then horrified.

"Trident! Your shoulder! What happened to your shoulder?" he asked.

"Somebody shot me," Trident moaned.

G.E. spun around with his weapon to his shoulder, scanned the horizon through his scope and then slowly pulled the rifle away as a realization dawned. This rifle was meant to do the same thing to people as it had to clay pigeons.

"Trident!" he said, coming to this conclusion.

"What?" he groaned.

"Trident! I think *I* shot you!"

"Then why did you shoot me, Gee?" Trident croaked.

"It was supposed to be a joke!"

Trident looked over to his shoulder as best he could, winced in pain.

"Oh," he said. "I get it." Trident began lifting himself to his feet and promptly fell back down again.

G.E. looked at the rifle in his arms and felt betrayed. Betrayed by Petrus, by Kat. By Sergeant Hildebrand and the entire Virtual Training Corps. It was one thing to be certain your aim was right and true, but there was no reason to make these rifles that dangerous, he concluded.

"Come on, man, I can take you somewhere where you can get help."

"I think I'm okay," Trident said and then fainted.

"You barely winged him," Kat said, producing a medical kit from her backpack.

Once Trident regained consciousness, he caught G.E. up on his Pepsicon experience.

"They said boot camp would be terrible and it was," Trident said between gasps as Kat dressed the wound. "But not this terrible." After a few exhaustive minutes and a small dose of morphine, Trident managed to stand on his feet. They made their way back to the road where Trident told the saga of his short experience as a marine.

"Did you get to finally fly a real copter?" G.E. asked.

"Don't think they even have any. And they don't even have Siege Systems. They have us play on this Chinese system. All the words are in some Chinese language that looks like tiny crossed-out squares and little flags. The game is about feeding a bunch of fat little furry creatures with big eyes. You have no idea how many of those stupid little beasts I had to feed. You run up to them and give them beams of colored light or dust them with stars until they poop. Then they'd leave behind a heart or a meat-bun or something stupid like that. Occasionally they leave behind something else, a raygun or a helmet that sparkles and you're ordered to immediately inform a superior officer if you get one. It could take all day to get just one, or all week they said, but getting those little sparkly bits—that was the whole point. They'll give you a little medal if you ever managed to get one to drop."

"Ever get one?" G.E. asked.

"Nah. When we got to take a break from the games, boot camp was all about running through tires, jumping over obstacles and following orders. I got to shoot a real gun once. But then they said we had to fight. The Buy-Net connection was sabotaged. They slapped guns in everybody's hands and sent us out the door."

"Was that part like the Siege Arena?" G.E. asked. The difference could be summed up in two words, really, or that was at least how simple the explanation was for Trident.

"Metal bits," he said with a deep sigh.

G.E. waited for more, but Trident just nodded and poked his finger into the barrel of G.E.'s Remington.

"Yeah, that's right. Little bits of metal fly out of this part here and, if they hit you, they punch a hole right through you!"

"I don't see why," G.E. said.

"I don't either. And that's not even the unfortunate part. Turns out this is what they are supposed to do. Punch holes in you. Turns out they are trying to kill you out there. So I said, 'I'd like to leave sir, before I get killed, please.'"

"And what did they tell you?"

"Tell me? Tell me? They drove us to a damn field full of this. Told us to run up the hill and shoot the guys on top. But the guys on top had much better guns, I could tell by how much faster they shot and how much louder they were. Plus, they had little explosions going off here and there. Most of the other recruits just put their head down and ran up the hill. I saw dozens of guys just like me, mowed down. The most lopsided rules I've ever seen and here I was in the center of it. They ran head-on into the fray, but I hooked around backwards." Tears began to well in Trident's eyes.

"You try to take the flank!" G.E said. "That's what I would have done!"

"They told me I'd be a pilot! I could have been a pilot! At least then I would have known how to fly my way out of a mess as bad as this...." He sighed. "But this...this was impossible."

"Did you tell them?"

"I wanted to," Trident sniffed. "I went to tell my CO, my commanding officer."

"And what did he tell you?"

"Well, I can't be certain," Trident said, short of breath and troubled by the memory. He shook his head.

"I think he may have been dead."

"Dead?"

"Yeah, he took some bits of metal to his chest. And his head. Yeah, I think a big bit of it hit him in the head."

"So?"

"So I just walked the other way. And after a while I found some help."

"From the Schwags!"

"From the Schwags, yeah."

"But they're mad!"

"Not the ones I came across. No different than the folks around here, really. I explained to this nice one that I had no intention to combat him."

"So how did you get back here?" G.E. asked.

"That same guy. Mitch was his name. I told him all I wanted to do was just go back home. After I explained the Supercenter, the X-2 Deep Space Shuttle, he became very sympathetic. He explained to me that he was actually an Astrophysicist. He said that if I traded my body armor and M-16 to him he would build me a rocket that would take me back to Buy-All.

"He built it out of this big black tire, closed it off on each side. It was a small vessel, and I was skeptical it could survive the vacuum of space, but he assured me it would work. I mean, I'm no rocket scientist myself. He crammed me into the tire and closed the lid. It was very dark inside. Then it started to move and rumble. It got going really fast at one point until at last it crashed into this pond. I flew out of the hatch. After the spinning went away, I found Mitch running down a hill to me.

"'Wow that was quite a ride!' Mitch said. 'So this is the planet you're from!' He picked up bits of junk on the shore and kept asking me what we called it. I told him Buy-All was a space station, that it should look more like aisles and check out counters, but he was certain we followed the correct flight trajectory. He even showed me a large map and a bunch of equations he'd drawn up on a brown paper grocery bag. He recovered the tire from the pond and complained about all the work he'd have to do to get it operational for interstellar travel again. So I handed off my armor and let him keep my rifle, good riddance.

"I started looking around for #1501. I walked for a long time without seeing a single soul. Just as I was thinking I hadn't really left Pepsicon, you shot me," Trident said, standing up. Dizzy from the injury, he at once slipped back to the ground.

"Okay, I remember that part."

At that instant, they were interrupted by a rumbling sound in the distance.

"The Merch Machine!" G.E. said. "It's happening right now!"

"Quick," Kat said. "Grab some branches."

# CHAPTER 17

## The Merchandise Machine

**Hildebrand was satisfied he'd killed** two birds with one stone. The first confirmed G.E. had committed treason and could be dismissed accordingly, without formal tribunal, the second identified the headquarters of the Cherry Glens Brigade. He drove his meager cache of two FIM-92A rockets down the winding access road leading away from the Supercenter. Taking out Cherry Glens might just get him back on the Central Command's good side, seeing their plan to convert #1501 to a munitions center had so far failed miserably. Things might just work out okay, he thought.

His DAGR device beeped with a message from Benson intended to reveal the location of the Cherry Glens insurgent base camp. He pulled up the coordinates, but he did not recognize the landscape. He zoomed out to the city level.

"Tixmul...Chumoox... El Corozo?" Hildebrand read, trying to keep one eye on the road. He zoomed out further to find he was examining the geography of the Yucatan Peninsula.

"Worthless," he grumbled to himself in the cab of the sixteen wheeler. He clipped the DAGR to his belt and took a long pull from his Café Guerre Soy Mocha Latte. As the white lid descended from his view, what he saw blocking

the road ahead sent hot coffee from out his mouth and onto
the console of the rig. He slammed the brakes and the truck
rumbled to a halt just before colliding with a blockade of
hastily stacked brush. Two soldiers knelt behind it, rifles
trained in his direction. Hildebrand then heard a whistle to
his left. He looked out the side window and found Trident,
waving with one arm, the other in a sling. He rolled down
the window.

"Come on out, sir," Trident began. "It's safe."

Hildebrand pulled the emergency brake and shut off the
engine. The forest was eerily quiet in the sudden absence of
the churning diesel engine.

Kat stepped from out of the brush.

"Hands behind your head!" she ordered as she marched
to him. "On your knees!"

G.E. slung the Remington over his shoulder and hurried
to catch up.

"Kat! No!" he said. "It's cool. That's just Sarge. He's harmless." Upon recognizing his former recruit, Hildebrand let
out a long groan, letting his hands fall from atop his head and
over his face.

"I'm serious! Hands behind your head!" She examined the
truck as she kept her rifle on the Sergeant. G.E. inspected the
truck as well, attempting to determine its role in merchandise
creation. This was made abundantly clear when Kat lifted the
trailer door to reveal the familiar merch room, exactly as G.E.
remembered it. The entire trailer was empty, save two long
wooden boxes strapped down in the center.

"What are these?" Kat demanded. Hildebrand dropped
his arms from behind his head and sighed. Kat popped the

latches and lifted the lid to reveal a long, green FIM-92A rocket set inside crisp foam casing.

"Holy crap!" She jumped back. "I've never seen anything like this!"

"Well, congratulations, Westinghouse," Hildebrand said. "You've finally won now, haven't you? You've betrayed the Corps, undermined your Supercenter, escaped, joined forces with the enemy, and hijacked a weapons shipment."

"It only sounds impressive when you put it that way," G.E. said. "Don't worry, sir. The Cherry Glens Brigade will help us. If we can convince them of the danger, then surely they will join us in our conflict with the Schwags of Pepsicon."

As G.E. and Trident also turned to marvel at the impressive rocket launcher within, Hildebrand seized the opportunity. He slowly reached down to the DAGR device on his belt and activated the emergency tracking beacon.

"Well, let's get these back to base and show this to Lieutenant Petrus," Kat said. "You." She pointed at Hildebrand. "Grab a handle." Without being asked, G.E. took the other side of the rocket case and together they carried it to the Cherry Glens Headquarters.

Trident made small talk along the way. "Trees here are just like the ones on Pepsicon." Kat kept her rifle poised on Hildebrand as she imagined what reward may be in store for such a find as this.

"Just like this, huh?" G.E. asked.

"Yup."

"I'll be."

Hildebrand let out an exasperated sigh. "You two are some real frickin' brain surgeons. Anyone ever tell you that?"

"No sir," said G.E.

"No sir," said Trident.

"Just shut up about Pepsicon, okay?"

"Yessir," they said in unison.

They reached camp without another word. The refugees of Cherry Glens stirred when they saw the uniformed sergeant being led to camp.

"Get him out of here!" shouted one of the refugees, concerned that one Federalist soldier would lead to more in the area.

Kat led them into the chapel map room. Petrus noted Trident's pale skin, just like both G.E. and the strange Mennonite from earlier that morning. He did not appreciate having his strategic planning interrupted for a second time that day, but judging by the appearance of Hildebrand, his decorated uniform and impeccable drill hat, Petrus began to suspect there might be something serious to all this Buy-All business after all.

"We captured them both while out on patrol," Kat offered proudly.

"So," Petrus began. "I take it the Military is coming here to offer support in our campaign against Walden Meadows?"

"I don't think so," Trident answered. "That is, I don't know how much help we'd be. Schwaggies steamrolled us just the other day."

"Yeah," added G.E. "We have been at war with them for years. You guys just don't know what kind of threat they are."

"Years, eh?" Petrus said. "I too have been at war for a number of years. What an odd coincidence."

Hildebrand did not like where the self-appointed

Lieutenant was going with this and could not remain quiet any longer.

"He's right." Hildebrand turned to address Petrus. "We *are* all on the same side. This soldier of yours, this G.E., happens to be a highly valuable fugitive of the US government. Your cooperation in turning him over to the proper authorities will no doubt result in your esteemed recognition. We could overlook all this insurrection nonsense you have going on here. I'm talking about promotion. Your own battalion. No more chipping in from the rough. You might actually have a chance to do something to win this war."

"What? You mean the big one, with Dixie?" asked Petrus.

"No," G.E. corrected him. "The aliens. Pepsicon. The Schwags." He waved his hands in the air dismissively. "It's light years away."

"That so?" Petrus' eyes fixed on Hildebrand. "Perhaps you would like to explain why this kid keeps talking about war with extra-terrestrials?"

Trident added, "I don't know if they're aware you guys are fighting each other here."

"Enough!" Hildebrand shouted. "This is your last chance." He jerked a thumb at G.E. and Trident. "Stop listening to these two deserters and do something for your country—"

Petrus perked up at once. G.E.'s story suddenly made sense. "Wait. Did you say *deserters*?" Petrus once and for all realized at that moment where G.E. originated from. Impossible, bizarre as it would seem, if he had indeed absconded from the Federalist forces, and if he claimed to hail from a giant big-box retail store, then perhaps these buildings had been repurposed for just such an activity.

"Private Conrad," he announced.

"Yessir?" Conrad jumped to his feet.

"Open a radio communiqué. All channels."

"Don't do it," Hildebrand mumbled as his hand crept to the DAGR on his belt. Conrad stepped over to the HAM radio, flicked a number of switches and turned a dial.

"Good to go sir." He pushed the microphone to Petrus.

"Attention all units, this is Lieutenant Dmitri Petrus of the Cherry Glens Brigade. Now, you might not find us allies at the present moment, but you will agree with at least this much. We all share a common enemy. And if you find the Federalist Occupation of Southeast Missouri as much a pain in the ass as we, you'll listen up. We have obtained classified information pertaining to Federalist bases within purportedly neutral territory. Find and target all Buy-All Supercenters. I repeat, focus—"

Suddenly and without warning the room shook from the sound of a tremendous explosion. The stained glass shattered and a ceiling beam fell, crushing the map table and radio. Kat poked her head out of the chapel doors and saw a tiny white triangle flit across the sky.

"Drone!" she yelled and was immediately shoved aside by a fleeing Sergeant Hildebrand. He squeezed his DAGR, which commanded the drone plane to assault the chapel a second time. The small plane circled around, whistled overhead, and dropped a line of cluster bombs along a route that overlapped the camp. G.E. and Trident tumbled to the floor as the chapel shook with the impact of a second strike. Guns were distributed to everyone. Sufficiently armed, the Cherry Glens Brigade deployed to the roof of the church. Petrus and the others climbed the stairs just in time to see the church marquee explode. They lined up along the crenellated bunker wall and aimed into the distance.

"Fire at will!" Petrus yelled, and then the bunker filled with the sound of rifle reports. G.E. lifted his fingers to his ears, forearms clutching the Remington to his chest.

"What the hell are you two waiting for!" Petrus yelled at G.E. and Trident. "Fire! Fire!"

G.E. threw his arms up and let the Remington fall to the floor. Trident did the same, his weapon striking the floor with a soft clunk.

"What are you two doing?" Petrus yelled as he ducked behind the sandbag wall. Brass bullet shells filled the air like confetti as the other soldiers tried in vain to track and lead the agile target. "This is treason! You can't just abandon this outfit!"

"Yeah," Trident said, pointing to his shoulder. "I've already gone today." And with that he stepped down the stairwell.

"Besides, this won't work!" G.E. yelled. "You can't use a Light Rifle on a plane!" This was of course a lesson based on the ground rules of the Siege Arena, which, in this case happened to coincide with reality, as the plane was well reinforced with Kevlar, not to mention moving at speeds nearly impossible to lead with a bullet. Then he too disappeared down the steps leading back to the chapel.

"Damn Mennonite pacifists!" Petrus shook his fist.

"Sir?" Kat paused from firing at the swooping aircraft.

G.E. soon returned to the roof, this time with the FIM-92A slung over his shoulder.

"This is the last time," he shouted to Petrus.

G.E. activated the launcher. A tiny LCD screen flipped open, turned on, and flashed a green grid over a video image of the horizon beyond the chapel. G.E. quickly honed in on the solitary aerial target just as it turned toward them for another bombing run. The rocket burst out of the launcher and an enormous tongue of fire spat from the rear. The drone was smart enough to recognize it was being chased by an incoming rocket and it veered toward the sun to evade and hopefully confound the rocket's tracking system. But the FIM-92A was slightly more advanced. After a series of impressively choreographed evasive maneuvers, the battle of microprocessor wits ended with a fantastic explosion, the drone careening downward in a ball of flame.

# CHAPTER 18

➲ **The Return**

**Seventeen years ago, Cherry Glens** resident Abraham Strong purchased a variable-speed cordless drill from Buy-All Supercenter #1501 and returned it after installing new cabinets in his kitchen. What's the harm in returning a drill he had only used for a few minutes? he figured. Now, seventeen years later, a military aerial drone, shot down by an FIM-92A surface-to-air rocket manufactured at the exact same Buy-All Supercenter where he had unscrupulously purchased and returned the drill, suddenly and without warning crashed through his patio door. The flaming wreckage savaged each and every one of the cabinets of his kitchen, leaving the entire home a blazing inferno. Abraham Strong fleeing the scene, miraculously unscathed, failed to appreciate this circuitous reprisal.

Sergeant Hildebrand managed to escape in the ensuing chaos, out of the undeveloped track of forested land and into the affluent subdivision. Lieutenant Petrus sent Kat, G.E., and Trident to track down Hildebrand's rig along Highway 63, but not without first pinning a tiny brass Boy Scout *Webelos* pin to G.E.'s chest, commemorating his valiant defeat of the aerial drone.

When they arrived, all three climbed into the cab of the truck. Trident took the wheel, having been acquainted with its controls after ample Siege Arena vehicular training. Operating the vehicle one-handed due to his injury, he did his best to turn the giant rig around, dropping the trailer into a ditch beside the road.

"Careful...Careful..." Trident said as the trailer smashed young saplings and brambles beside the road. The truck rocked up and down on creaking suspension as it rumbled out of the ditch. At last, the behemoth faced back toward the direction it had come.

"Okay, Trident. This road should feed into the Supercenter. I remember seeing flooring like this in Outlot B," G.E. explained.

As the truck rolled forward, Kat bounced excitedly on the springy bench seat, taking off her hat and shaking her hair out. She hung her torso out of the window and watched the Cherry Glen's church steeple recede into the distance behind them.

"I can't believe we're doing this. Stealing a truck!" She leaned back on the seat and clapped G.E. on his thigh. "Way more exciting than stupid recon hikes."

The truck pressed onward despite Trident grinding the clutch as he attempted to transpose the combination of game pad buttons to the arrangement of pedals and levers around him.

Only a few hundred yards away, deep in the forest beside them, one Edward Benson heard the roar of the truck engine as he continued to struggle with his DAGR, now desperate just to find his way back to Buy-All Supercenter #1501.

"Kat. The Supercenter. Where is it?" G.E. asked.

"Oh, I don't know. Just keep going and we'll find it eventually," she said, parroting G.E.'s earlier brazen confidence and simply enjoying the ride. They continued down the service road that quickly led well outside the implied boundaries of the Cherry Glens Brigade. They rolled unceremoniously up the entry ramp of Highway 63, the double-lane highway decrepit and untraveled. Mostly untraveled. Intermittent campfires smoldered at unknown distances off the road. They passed through Prescott, wincing as they slammed over gigantic potholes, swerving around long-abandoned automobiles and their jettisoned cargo— furniture mostly, construction equipment, or, as they found upon entering Licking city limits, a snarl of shattered two-by-fours, apparently unworthy of reclamation.

G.E. attempted to measure the distance traveled in Supercenter units and came to the conclusion they were so impossibly far away that a return to camp was now ruled out entirely. What he did not know was that Petrus and the other Cherry Glens Brigadiers had received word from Walden Meadows confirming the existence of military installations within abandoned retail Supercenters, and they too were now en route to the Supercenter, having taken the trail he and Kat traveled the day before.

His first estimates of the Merchandise Machine had already been exceeded a thousand-fold, but he returned to his composition book nonetheless. As he wrote, they passed another of the many local militias supposedly protecting their own suburban neighborhood from rival subdivisions. A group of men carried their subdivision entrance plaque all the way to the side of the highway.

A slate merestone, letters carved in gothic script, displayed the name of the nearby subdivision turned sovereign nation—Whispering Meadow Estates. They had set up an improvised checkpoint along the highway in order to shake down travelers, but when they saw the military colors painted along the trailer, they kept their distance. Their heads turned to watch as the sixteen-wheeler dodged around more potholes and debris scattered along the highway. The men nodded and waved, having grown accustomed to seeing this vehicle pass through before, one time even hauling a large carnival rocket.

Thick, deciduous forest rolled over rounded hillsides. The Ozark Mountains were subtle, hidden under a canopy of green, save occasional streaks of chiseled limestone cliffs overlooking rivers and creeks. Averaging no more than twenty miles an hour, they followed a circuitous route through Licking. They saw for the first time upright power lines, fenced livestock, and the occasional fruit vendor along the highway. Upon reaching the far side of town, the familiar gray rectangle of Supercenter #1501 at last came into view. Trident dodged the truck around the bulldozed remains of the highway overpass and down the service road that snaked behind the Supercenter.

The graveled, rear parking area was just as G.E. remembered it. Unfortunately, also just as Trident remembered the rocket's landing zone upon Pepsicon as well.

"Dammit," Trident said, realizing at last what he had been incrementally suspecting ever since his arrival to this strange place—that Pepsicon and Buy-All were one in the same. He did not dwell on this long. "So, what now, then?" he asked as they slowly approached the Shuttle Bay door.

G.E. studied the docking zone, hatching a plan while

inside the voice of Edward Benson sounded over the P.A. Having now completely given up hope of tracking down the absconded associate, Benson patched into the system remotely and issued a statement via the DAGR device. The still unrelenting drumbeat of associates wound down as Benson's voice boomed overhead.

"We at Supercenter #1501 were stunned to discover that over the course of the past few months our intrepid Siege Arena hero G.E. Westinghouse worked diligently to uncover a sinister Schwagist plot to overthrow our Supercenter. Uncertain how far the Schwagist corruption infected the management of the Supercenter, he took justice into his own hands and commandeered a flight to Pepsicon. I report to you now from that very battlefield with good news. G.E. was victorious!"

The Supercenter burst into cheers. The associates quieted, waiting to hear if G.E. had indeed brought peace to Pepsicon and ended the war. Just as Benson began to speak again, the signal from the deep Missouri wilderness suddenly cut out. Their patience now expired, the associates returned to their revelry, dancing, and cavorting throughout the Supercenter.

"My fellow Associates," Benson continued, alone in the wilderness and unaware he spoke into a dead DAGR. "Led by myself, the Army deployed a rescue unit to Pepsicon at once. I regret that although our hero G.E. single-handedly defeated a key cell of Primitivist forces, G.E. Westinghouse of Supercenter #1501 was killed in action on that fateful day." Though Benson was well off-script, the remainder of Tile Melt he had taken helped him through the speech and emboldened him.

"G.E. Westinghouse was an inspiration on and off the Siege Arena, as with all who have made the ultimate sacrifice in the war against Primitivism." Benson nodded with satisfaction and looked down at the DAGR phone only to find the LCD screen had turned to a solid tan rectangle. "Crap!" he yelled and pressed the power button to no avail. As he shook the unit, the subject of his announcement stood outside the roll-up cargo doors, Hildebrand's keychain in hand.

# CHAPTER 19

→ **Prophecy Fulfilled**

**Benson smacked the DAGR in** his hand, but this did nothing to generate additional battery power. After walking just a few more minutes, he spotted a row of shimmering vehicles obscured between tree trunks in the distance.

He pushed through the thicket and, once escaping its stifling brambles, found a gravel access road leading to a campground within Mark Twain National Forest. The line of cars numbered in the dozens, as far as his eye could see. He followed them down the road, hoping to find at least one occupied, but it was clear by the deflated tires that these vehicles had been here for a very long time. Old school busses and RVs were covered in frayed, illegible stickers or decorated in ribbons of spray paint. On the back of a green school bus, somebody had written "honk at us!" in black magic marker. And again on the side, somebody had added, "on the road again," "strangers stopping strangers," and "did you remember to honk?" Benson knocked on windows lined with curtains, but found each vehicle unoccupied. He could smell a fire burning in the distance. After passing by a dozen busses and vans, he saw somebody drop down from a school bus emergency exit.

A man wearing only heavily patched khaki shorts, a thick, hemp braided necklace, and a shaggy beard froze, looked up

from the ground, and locked eyes with Benson. Benson's expression turned at once from ecstatic to horrified. No doubt
about it—this man was a crust punk. Though the planet
Pepsicon was very much a ruse, and though he himself had
greatly exaggerated Schwagism's threat, it was now clear to
Benson the prophecy had at last come to pass.

Benson staggered toward the figure, still frozen and
staring.

"Batteries? Batteries?" Benson mumbled as he approached. The man looked him up and down and then stumbled backwards. He caught his balance and raised a horrified
hand to his mouth.

"Babylon! Babylon!" The man cried out and sprinted
away, falling over himself to escape.

Benson ran after him. Other figures emerged from behind vehicles parked along the road. A girl wearing a black
canvas smock shouted at him. Benson lost track of the man
he chased and stopped to catch his breath. The girl approached him, staring with fear and awe, and he could see
she was, in fact, wearing pants, but the middle part of her
blue jeans was nothing but holes. All that was left of the
middle were strips of denim that ran down the sides of her
legs to a pair of functionless cuffs. Stray dogs circled at a distance, panting and sickly. The air grew thick with the smell
of smoke. A man stuck his head out of the window of a black
spray-painted bus.

"Namasté!" he said warmly and then found his way outside the bus.

A hand appeared from behind Benson and yanked the
scarf from around his neck. He spun around to find himself

surrounded by five men and women, all marveling at his outfit, particularly his boots. None wore shoes of their own and, judging by their blackened toes, Benson trusted they hadn't for some time. He was reminded of J.R.R. Tolkien's *Lord of the Rings* trilogy. At the time he read the books, he had found it specious that the hero Frodo could get from his Shire backyard to Mordor without a pair of shoes, but from the looks of the feet of those surrounding him, they had done exactly that and more.

One of the men carefully pulled the aviator sunglasses from Benson's face. He put them on and the others all laughed.

Benson blinked in the sunlight. Smoke burned his eyes. He mumbled something about ultraviolet rays, but they offered no response.

"Come," the man from the bus window said. They led Benson off into the woods. Not far from where they started, Benson found a group of eight more digging an enormous hole the size of a swimming pool with their bare hands. A row of dirty men sat along the lip of the hole, watching others sling dirt from the bottom, perhaps waiting their turn. Another pair stripped bark from cedar logs with rocks and assembled them into a table. The smell of smoke grew stronger, but Benson saw no sign of a campfire.

A girl seated on the edge of the hole looked at Benson with ravenous eyes as she dipped blackened fingers into a tin cup of cold chicken noodle soup and dropped the soggy noodles into her mouth.

The man from the school bus window clapped his hands once and everyone stopped. He motioned to Benson.

"Namasté, Brother Maftir." This was the tribal nickname

invented for Benson at that moment. Everyone lifted their hands and wriggled their fingers as a sign of approval.

"Namasté," the crowd whispered in unison.

"What are you going to do with the hole?" Benson asked nervously. His eyes burned. Everyone smiled.

"Sit down and kick it," one of them said, like it was painfully obvious to everyone but Benson.

He saw a crude sign made of flimsy cardboard tied to a tree with a piece of torn cloth. In black magic marker the name of the campsite was printed—Sit Down and Kick It.

At that moment, a man dressed entirely in black emerged from the woods and joined the circle that formed around the Supercenterintendent. Benson had a hard time recognizing him, given the full beard, but the small skullcap confirmed exactly what he suspected.

"Saul!" Benson whispered. "Saul! It's a miracle I've found you! For the love of God, you have to lead me away from this terrible place!"

The crowd whispered amongst themselves. Saul Zhener could not believe his eyes. He lifted his hand up, settling the crowd.

"The love of God, you say? Brother Semikhah," he called out. The man in the khaki shorts Benson earlier frightened stepped forward with his head bowed. "Thou shalt...." Saul rolled his hand forward, encouraging him to speak.

"Thou shalt not take the name of the Lord thy God in vain." The crowd then chanted in unison with him as they continued their digging.

"*For the Lord will not hold him guiltless that taketh his name in vain,*" they said together.

"Very good, brother Semikhah. Very good everyone. This man is clearly possessed by the Yetzer Ra. But we can help him. We can show him the path. Do we," asked Saul Zhener, "forgive Brother Maftir for his transgression against our Commandments?"

Saul smiled warmly at Benson and placed a hand upon his head.

Benson fell to his knees and began to sob softly. Instinctively, the others stopped digging and shaving logs at once. They slowly turned and moved toward him with outstretched arms. With a look of sheer terror on his face as he knelt before the hole, the group closed in on Benson with hugs.

# CHAPTER 20

## The Best Laid Plans

**Another first Tuesday of the** month and with it another batch of merchandise arrived at Buy-All Supercenter #1501. Huck drove the forklift to the docking room gate, stepped off, and lifted the door. A printed pink carbon copy manifest hung from the inside wall of the trailer. Just like every other associate in the Supercenter, he believed it simply materialized into being over the course of the past month.

At once, his eyes were drawn to a single line amended to the bottom of the manifest in hand-written green ink.

"For...immediate...delivery," he read. Huck let out a sigh, looked at his watch, and then proceeded to unpack the trailer, beginning with this first item.

Not far away, in the Education Department, Nestlé watched a woman on a screen lecture her and the other five students around her on economics.

"The more popular a product, the lower its ultimate cost. As the manufacturing machine produces more of this item, the more quickly the set-up costs are amortized. We call this *economies of scale*. This is why popular artists such as Shelly Arkansas can offer their music at such a low price. After the costs of production are recouped, the duplication of MP3s for your All-Pod players is, well, it's practically free. It's just data." The woman hesitated, her eyes darted left and right as a grin curled the corners of her mouth. She continued *sotto voce*, "Not that this should encourage you to pirate your music." A voice was heard off camera, and she turned her head to face it.

"Whatever, Ed," the voice interrupted her a second time. "Fine, Ed, why don't you just edit it out, hotshot?" The children looked at one another, confused. "Moving on," she continued, "the tenants of commerce teach us that vertical proliferation within a market leads to overwhelming profit due to—"

The video paused and the children pulled off their headsets. Nestlé looked around her and found Huck standing over the learning kiosk.

"Nestlé Novartis?" he asked.

Nestlé raised a slender arm.

"Sign here." He thrust the clipboard toward her. "Just anywhere."

As she printed her name on the bottom of the pink carbon copy, she gingerly stepped around the forklift and let out a faint squeal. An enormous six-foot plush bear sat on a palette before her. The other children gasped one by one as they too discovered this prize.

"All yours, kid," Huck said. He dragged it from the palette and set it before her. "Good luck getting that into your compartment."

"Wow," Nestlé said. She lifted one of its arms, dropped it back down. Little Debbie stepped forward and touched Nestlé's elbow.

"Wait, Nestlé. There's a note around his neck," her friend whispered.

Nestlé slipped a rolled up sheet of notebook paper out from a simple ribbon loop. She unrolled the note and read it aloud.

"Clap thrice to bring me to life," she read. Her eyes widened to saucers. She looked back at the other children for a moment, tucked the note under her arm. One, two, three claps and the bear leapt from the floor.

The children squealed with alarm and delight. Those closest scurried behind the farthest until a sharp half-circle formed around the giant, animated bear. The bear stood for a long moment, looking at them all, and then, not knowing what else to do, burst into dance. It ran in place, lifted its right arm, placed its left on its waist and pumped its hips. The children applauded. It ran in place some more, kicked its legs out, laid down on the tile, and attempted a backspin. Brett, filling in for Benson as a way of making amends for distributing Tile Melt, saw the commotion and pushed his way through the kids.

"Okay, that's enough. Nestlé, you can take your toy back home now," he said.

The bear stopped, hung its head in shame, and looked at Brett. The bear raised its hands and stepped menacingly toward Brett in big, hulking steps. Brett stepped backwards nervously. The bear grasped its head in his hands and then lifted it from its shoulders to reveal the face of G.E. within.

"Gee!" Nestlé yelled, and ran to hug him. Huck leapt from the seat of his forklift and rushed to do the same.

"Hey everybody," Huck yelled at the top of his lungs. "Gee's back!"

Associates gathered around the border of the Education Department. Huck grabbed G.E.'s arm and pulled G.E. to the forklift. Nestlé tightly attached to his furry waist. G.E. waved to the onlookers as Huck placed him on the palette and then activated the lift, raising G.E. and Nestlé into the air. Yellow light spinning atop the forklift, he drove them slowly from the Education Department and down Center Aisle, a procession gathering behind them.

"Stop here," G.E. said once they reached the scarred foyer at the front of the Supercenter.

G.E. pulled his arms inside the torso of the stuffed bear and grimaced as he fished around. Bits of Styrofoam pellets spilled to the floor. At last, G.E. retrieved his CB radio.

"Kat? Do you read me?" he spoke.

"Roger that, G.E. We are ready in position. Awaiting your signal."

"Okay. All clear from this side. Let 'er rip."

At that moment, a concussive boom issued from beyond the Supercenter, and a flash came from the vestibule. Heads turned and discovered the now splintered and broken decades-old two-by-fours and metal panels that sealed the foyer off from the outside world.

Another loud report sounded throughout the Supercenter. With it, the first rays of sunlight broke through, accompanied by a thin veil of dust and smoke. After a few seconds, the dust settled to reveal a pair of soldiers dressed in camouflage, pushing aside debris and clearing the entryway.

One by one, dazed associates stepped across laminated shards of shatterproof glass. They stepped along the concrete sidewalk beside the tarnished steel carousel horse and meandered into the vast asphalt parking lot. There, Brigadiers and refugees of Cherry Glens greeted them.

Before long, the entirety of the Supercenter filled the parking lot. G.E. was the last to exit. He watched as they shook hands and greeted one another. He turned and looked at the twisted, wretched entryway blown into the front of the Supercenter, never to be sealed again. As he stared into the dark empty chasm, a figure appeared and stepped out into the light. It was a tiny person, only three feet in height, shielding his eyes from the sun. The tiny man approached G.E. and held out his hand.

"I have looked forward to the day we would finally meet," the little man said. "But I never supposed it would take this for it to finally happen. Sam Torino. A pleasure." He bowed slightly.

G.E. offered a handshake, but found his hand occupied by Hildebrand's key chain. As he looked down at it, he noticed for the first time several other keys, each marked with a different number. G.E. hurriedly flipped through the series of keys until at last coming upon the one he sought. Stamped into the brass, a hash mark followed by a four-digit number.

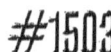

We hope you've enjoyed the story. Please help us share this story with other readers by letting us know what you thought with a review on either **amazon.com** or **goodreads.com**.

Thank you kindly,
Montag Press Collective

# AN INTERVIEW WITH JASON RIZOS

Conducted by Douglas Lain, November 13, 2012

*From where did the idea for* Supercenter *come?*
Two things sparked my imagination. First, a line delivered
by James Howard Kunstler in *The End of Suburbia* caught
my attention. He says something to the effect that in the
future we will have all of these big-box retail stores and
they aren't conducive to re-purposing. I thought, well, if we
had to repurpose retail stores in a time of crisis, we would
probably use them as residential housing. But what if you
can't exactly bulldoze these gargantuan structures? Second,
one day as I was driving my car through the neighborhood
in which I grew up, I came to a precipice where the arterial
Manchester Road intersects Ries Road. I had a vantage of
all this suburban sprawl, chain restaurants, strip malls, car
dealerships, the usual stuff, but it became so overwhelmingly
intimidating that I just wanted out. I had to run out, which

is a feeling that usually comes over me suddenly when inside a mall after I reach a certain threshold. They say malls are designed with a casino-esque incongruity, meant to dazzle and mesmerize the senses; they even have a term for this: a *Gruen Transfer*. I think when it starts to take hold of me I get a claustrophobic reaction. I kind of say, "I have to get out of here. Now." Well, I had this sensation for the first time *outdoors*. It occurred to me that we've managed to cultivate our entire environment to mimic retail shopping so utterly completely that residents of this community of Ballwin, Missouri, can essentially live their entire lives, home, job, recreation, in an all-consuming shopping mall. How sad is that? This is how it looks everywhere in suburban America. The more affluent the residents are, the more ubiquitous the retail. This is the ultimate urban utopia we have created for ourselves—pure retail immersion. Hell with it, I thought, if they love their shopping so much, why don't they just move in?

**Do you think the Big Box stores will continue to be the dominate force they are today in the future? Do you see this book staying front and center or are stores like Wal-Mart crumbling?**

I think it's going to be front and center. I set the book up as a proposition that says in the future when all other vestiges of capitalist society erode, this is the last one that will remain because it's the one we elevate the most and has the most staying power. End-game Capitalism dictates that as the speciation of commerce goes away, by consolidation, you've got these corporations merging, giving consumers fewer and fewer options. Compare it to an ecosystem that is in peril. All you are left with is a couple of specialized species. That's what I see in Big Box retailers; they have the power to withstand economic crisis and environmental crisis. A tornado cutting through Arkansas is not going to wipe out Wal-Mart. So yeah, I see them as being around forever.

*Do you think they'll be around even after you release your book? Do you think you are going to do some damage with this?*
I wish they'd carry in their stores. I'd be obsequious towards Wal-Mart. People often ask me why I hate Wal-Mart so much, but I say I'm not here to debate that. That's the difference with storytelling; people resonate with stories. I just want to do the whole holding a mirror up thing. If this is the kind of contemporary society you want to celebrate, then this is the future I see for you. It's not the bad future; it's just the future.

*So, in your book, it turns out the society that supports Wal-Mart has collapsed. Do you think that Capitalism and Wal-Mart are so strong that they can sustain themselves?*
I do. The way we have insinuated ourselves into consumer capitalism, we are like addicts. We would let our lives crumble, we would live in a gutter with poor hygiene before we'd let go of our habits. In this future society, the only thing that's left is the military and the Big Box Supercenter. Unfortunately, they have a little bit of a symbiotic relationship where the store provides the military with children for the military to fight their war, and the military

provides protection. What is more important than that, though, is the illusion: keeping the illusion that America is still strong so long as this place is still there and so long as people can shop and have that way of life and can pick things off the shelves and continue to get cheap crap imported from China. So long as we can preserve that, we've preserved something special.

**Did you come to write this book because you were a Wal-Mart shopper?**
Yeah, I have to confess. A little bit. This was surprisingly therapeutic, writing this, because I didn't realize just how much of a Wal-Mart brand consumerist I was, though my wife has no illusions about this. I grew up in the Midwest. You might not realize how ubiquitous Wal-Mart is in small towns. Especially when you are a kid, when Wal-Mart is like paradise. For me, writing *Supercenter* was an eye-opening experience.

**Do you ever feel like you're one of the kids sleeping on the shelves at a Wal-Mart?**
I got that from Pinocchio. I really like that story. They have the Land of Toys, which became Pleasure Island in the Disney film. They are in this dreamland, and that's much of *Supercenter* – let's create a dreamland where everybody has what they want, candy sugary cereals, and video games. I wanted to make the Land of Toys real, sustainable; we can achieve it! We can get everything taken care of for us, and the only thing the adults who supervise us care about is that we play more video games.

*But it's not sustainable. The reality is that eventually the Supercenter will be destroyed by the dystopia outside. They don't have any sustainable relationship with the rest of the world, supported by the military and force. In your story, there are no consumers left.*

There are only these people who are coerced into consumerism, right. This is just another reflection of what I see in our world. We have these insular little local economies where people are employed by Wal-Mart, and when they get off work, they just go shopping at Wal-Mart. It's this negative feedback loop that eventually leads to collapse, so yeah, it's not sustainable. You've corrected me there, but in relative terms, to some of our other institutions, it seems sustainable.

*Do you see* Supercenter *becoming a movie? Who would you like to direct it?*

Sure. Alex Payne. Or Terry Gilliam, if he's available. People say *Supercenter* is really cinematic, that I must have had a movie in mind, but maybe I have to confess that I just think in movies? Maybe that's an affectation of my generation's imagination. Montag Press also expressed interest in adaptation of *Supercenter*.

*What is it that appalls you most about Wal-Mart and why did you choose them as your model?*

There is no one like them. They are peerless in the world of retail, and their strategy is shameless. Like I said, I don't want to criticize them necessarily. They just do what they do; they're not any more evil than a shark doing what it does. But some of it was personal. In the college town I went to, in Columbia, Missouri, they had a Wal-Mart at Providence and Nifong boulevard. This was 1996. They had a Wal-Mart in one part of town, and they decided, "Oh, we could do better if we opened up on the other side of town." So they shut down this Wal-Mart and they just emptied the building. First of all, they were the ones to purvey the idea in Big Box retail to make buildings as cheap as possible, so it's just four walls of cinder block and this cheap roof. They just picked up and left this empty carcass of a building, this husk, and brought blight. Therefore, it destroyed this strip mall it was a part of, the adjacent little nail salons and all that were wiped out; this whole area of town just sunk. On the other side of town, the Wal-Mart was doing well until they decided to move it a second time. I guess it's obvious, they want to obliterate non-Wal-Mart retail, and once it's gone, it doesn't come back. People just drive a whole lot farther to shop.

*So they leave these turds, when they leave.*
And how do you reclaim that? Aside from bulldozing it, what do you do with ten acres of blacktop? Everyone laments the loss of quaint small business to Wal-Mart, but accepts it as a necessary outcome of the Free-Market Economy. Since Wal-Mart employs a huge swath of the town residents and because there really isn't anywhere else to go for shopping for essentials—groceries, toilet paper, pharmaceuticals, or even luxury goods, the employees wind up doing all of their shopping at Wal-Mart. At this point, a massive hunk of the town's economy is controlled by Wal-Mart. If Wal-Mart wished to double everybody's salary, they could, in turn, double all the prices, they could control the ebb and flow of

inflation and deflation, and within the bubble of that town's economy, it wouldn't matter to that bubble. In that sense, it seems like low wages would only force Wal-Mart to charge less for products and that they would raise wages to increase profitability, sort of like Henry Ford deliberately paying his workers enough to themselves buy a Model T; otherwise, who else would buy it?

Of course, Wal-Mart is a global entity. The externalities of the small town are what's important here. Wal-Mart can drive down wages and limit employees to part-time hours so severely that the workers become dependent on the government to provide welfare entitlements, such as food stamps and healthcare. That represents a massive savings for Wal-Mart, which relies on their employees being fed and medically cared for in order to work. That's an externality that essentially has American taxpayers subsidizing Wal-Mart's employee costs, not to mention subsidizing their shoppers, who are able to pay in food stamps that Wal-Mart exchanges for cash. I have a statistic from a government study that the average two-hundred employee Wal-Mart store costs the taxpayer $420,000 a year.

*Do you then think of yourself as a writer mostly as a polemicist? A satirist? A political writer? Or a storyteller first?*
When I first sat down, writing this as a satire, I found myself dressing up observations about what was then the late Bush administration, in allegory. Then, I realized that if my reader was solving these allegorical puzzles, fascinating though they

are, they don't say all that much that can't otherwise just be said didactically. So yeah, I rewrote the book as a fun story.

*So the authors you admire, are they satirists?*
Sure. Like many writers, Vonnegut had a large influence on me, as did Tom Robbins and Hunter S. Thompson. Of course, the biggest influence on *Supercenter* has been George Saunders, who does things that are quirky, goofy, and surreal, but they are also politically biting and are often futuristic too.

*So you had this impulse to do thought experiments, to create allegories, but you also wanted as a storyteller to entertain and keep people engaged with your characters. Is that a difficult challenge for you? Or even for the writers you admire?*
It is. It's the problem with all satire and allegory, because often characters take a backseat to the ideas. This is true of science fiction a lot of the time, where it becomes idea porn, and the characters have to be simple and archetypal, so they can be moved like chess pieces, and go through making a statement.

*One of the nice things about your book is that you know enough to know that ideas and characters cannot be separated, and your ideas are embodied in your characters. Do you find in everyday life that you run into people who are maybe characters themselves that are influenced by ideas they don't even know they have? I mean, do you think that the separation between ideas, everyday life and*

*everyday personalities is an artificial division, or do you*
*think these things are more integrated than we know?*
Yes. It's one of those things I feel we are all contaminated by,
myself included. I'm a guilty party, so not to criticize people,
we are really contaminated by cultural capitalism and by
consumerism. I mean we admonish it here in Oregon, but
we don't realize just how susceptible we are to it. We take
certain things for granted. I can't tell you how many times
I tell people, "You know maybe Capitalism is the problem,"
and they say, "Oh come on! You can't get rid of Capitalism.
I have to go to work for a living, are you asking me to go
to work and just give away my services for free?" It's like,
people aren't able to think about another away of life. Just
the ubiquity of the Supercenter blinds us. Today, we live in
the Supercenter ourselves; our communities are predicated
on this. We bring that zero-sum transactional mentality
to so many of our relationships. Douglas Rushkoff's nonfiction book *Life Inc.* also had a huge impact on *Supercenter*
as I was writing it. He describes how a corporate mentality
has fostered divisions in our communities and everyday
interactions with one another, and how greed and a doctrine
of radical individualism has become automatic.

*I'm reminded of Plato's Allegory of the Cave, does this*
*figure into* Supercenter?
This is the thing we can't see beyond. We have been exposed
to this way of life for so long, and when you take somebody
out of it and bring them into the light—and this is the story
of the main character being brought into the light—they'll
reject it.

*So the Supercenter is Plato's Cave, right, and the outside world is the light, or enlightenment, but the outside world is this dystopia?*
It is. Yeah.

*Which is not the same as in Plato's Allegory.*
No. That was the case, but I subverted that. Tragically, that's the world we live in. Is that too harshly cynical?

*So what's the motivation for someone to leave the cave if outside is the nightmare?*
To break off the shackles – it's an experience we all go through growing up. It's ignorance as bliss. It's not easy to walk away from your television, video games, professional sports, all the modern bread and circuses. You're left a pretty miserable, despondent person. It's just that these distractions are so appealing, baroque, rich in stimuli.

*In your book, you write about the ways in which we fail to think about an alternative way to live, something outside the Supercenter. Each way is unique, and each person has their own ability to deny the possibility of a different and better kind of life. Do you have the ambition to write a character who can think about an alternative way of life?*
The protagonist in Supercenter just wants to do right by what he knows, which is a flaw, but in the end he acts heroically. This occurs spontaneously from him being a good person, which is  partially redemptive.

*So even in someone who is enmeshed in the consumer
culture, there are these impulses...*

I think so, and that is represented in the psychedelic theme. If
you introduce the concepts of the psychedelic culture into any
society, no matter what it is, these preternatural, latent aspects of
the human psyche will come alive, eventually. There are certain
things that can't be repressed. You can try to repress them with
propaganda, video games, and consumerism. You can get those
things buried, but eventually they are going to percolate to the
surface and you are going to wind up with this. Oftentimes you
see a radical over-reaction, an over-reach, where people become
hypersensitive to consumerism. This is what I see us living
through right now, in our own community of Portland, Oregon.

*Video Games figure prominently into the story. Will wars
in the future be waged on computer screens?*

Mentioning this aspect of *Supercenter* to people was how I
first heard of *Ender's Game*. People also mention how the
US military is proliferating its drone strikes, essentially video
games for pilots halfway around the world in a domestic
military base. However, in *Supercenter* they are not meant
to be as sophisticated as that, or as Ender. They are simply
satisfactory cannon fodder. Part of *Supercenter* explores the
divorce between real and virtual violence, the "war is hell" parts
of war that are supposed to keep us from doing it all the time.

*And by making a game of it, you actually make war fun.*

War *is* fun, except for all the pain and suffering. What if we
could convince an enemy to have a paintball tournament for
control of a territory? People wonder why video games are

so violent. It's because the actual ballistic nature of combat is fun. The fact that the games are all about shooting and killing is really just an afterthought. The fact that Mario *dies* in Super Mario Brothers is just an artifact of putting the little bugger someplace he doesn't belong. I'm saying that we don't like these first person shooters because we sadistically get a thrill from murder. It's because the three-dimensional nature of aiming and shooting is fun, the guns and blood part is just to convey a sense of verisimilitude, as the best real-life analog to aiming and shooting is combat. Had we never invented guns or crossbows or bows and arrows, many video games would still be themed on throwing things at things.

### Is our society addicted to video games today?

I'm also interested in the role that virtual realms play in our current lives. People need to understand that video games are not like a drug, they are a drug. Playing a video game affects brain chemistry in an uncanny way, and the more immersive they become, the more profound the effect becomes. What would have been considered an appallingly pathological addiction fifteen years ago, say, playing video games for an eight hour stretch, several times a week, is now considered a reasonable hobby. People pour not only time, but actual intellectual energy to micro-economies and strategies for these complex realms, and the output of these systems is absolutely ephemeral.

People were awed by what television was able to do, insofar as pacifying the masses. Terence McKenna argued how and why television is literally a drug, by the way it affects brain chemistry and physiology, depressed heart rate, dilated eyes, etc. Video games take this several steps further. Add into the equation a moral cause, a noble crusade against a sworn enemy that seeks to destroy your very way of life, and voila.


*Links to Douglas Lain's blog, books, and podcast can be found at douglaslain.com*

Between fervent rounds of first-person-shooter games, risking his life on the Columbia river with a kite and surfboard, brewing homemade beer, and cynically decrying America's continued free fall into corporate fascism on his blog at Supercenternation.com, **Jason Rizos** plays a mild-mannered teacher of writing and literature at Portland Community College. He resides in Portland with his wife and two whippets of profoundly polarized intelligence capacity.

Prior to his teaching career, he deeply drank the cup of 9-to-5 malaise, occupying a cubicle for various unholy corporations in uninspired and despicable positions – as a technology sales representative, call center lackey, peddler of dangerous diet pills, and internet plagiarizer, to name a few. This is his first novel. He also writes short fiction and creative nonfiction, including a book on beer brewing hardware called *"The Frugal Homebrewer's Companion."*

His numerous awards and accolades would be listed here if he did not find doing so completely vain and if those awards existed. But this one time he went to graduate school and earned an MFA degree in fiction writing. Both this and his undergraduate degree went down in the Missouri University system, the state in which he was born and raised; St. Louis County. There, the strip malls and subdivisions go on for so long without reprieve and the sky can be so colorless from pollution that he once felt like he was driving his car through an indoor mall people lived in that went on forever and then decided he would write a book called Supercenter about this horrifying inclination so that others may share in the experience.

## Tree Black
Connor De Bruler

*It's hard being a trans woman. Harder still in North Carolina. Sandy Pogue knows this first-hand. Along with her Cherokee boyfriend Yona Bridger, Sandy manages to eke out a simple but happy life until inevitable circumstances force them to pack up and skip town.*

*As they try to carve out a new life, Sandy and Yona find themselves in the clutches of a bizarre cult of kidnapped women and demonic children. What is Yona's connection to this mysterious group of backwoods zealots, and can he help Sandy avoid a fate worse than death?*

**More than just their two lives hang in the balance as they hack a bloody swath through the ancient countryside, trying to reach the safety of the light through the TREE BLACK.**

*In **Tree Black**, de Bruler introduces the most amazing new heroine to blast onto the horror scene in ages. Swinging her hatchet through the heads of demon possessed hillbillies, Sandy is a cross between Hedwig and Evil Dead's Ash Williams. A fully realized and dynamic character instead of a boring clichéd archeytpe, Sandy strikes blow after brutal blow for outsiders everywhere.*

# ALSO FROM **MONTAG PRESS**

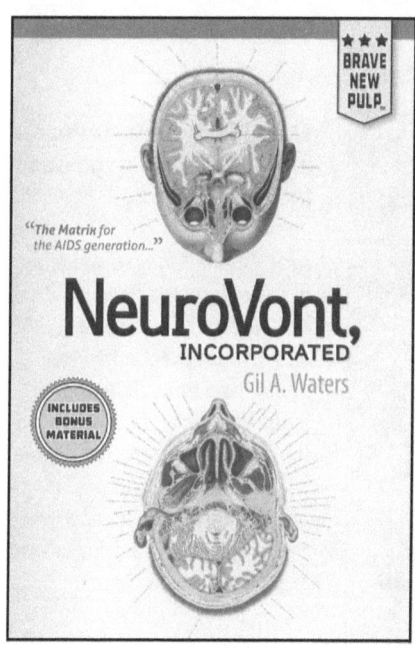

## NeuroVont, Incorporated
### Gil A. Waters

**Sex, drugs, and . . . post-corporeal transmigration?**

*Rik was stuck in a dead-end office job, relying on copious amounts of weed to make it through each day. His affair with the boss was the only highlight in his otherwise miserable existence. Then a terrorist group released a vicious, highly contagious virus—and everything changed.*

*When Rik becomes infected, he finds himself on the run from a government that ruthlessly hunts down anyone who might be sick. He soon learns that narcotics dull the symptoms, and that sex with another infected person gets him higher than he's ever been. He hooks up with a beautiful ex-government agent, Dez, who is also infected. Together, they seek sanctuary in a mysterious underground organization: NeuroVont, Incorporated. What they find will blow their minds…*

*Gil A. Waters' brisk and spare future perfect story imagines a world where getting infected means that you are chased by the government as bio-terrorists, and the only people that can help do so through an underground network of sex- and drug-fueled safe houses. As a beacon of hope,* **NeuroVont, Incorporated** *turns the cryptic anonymous corporation into a safe place where people in trouble can disappear to discover the true meaning of the infection that's sweeping America in the near future. The writing is light and cheery as Gil Waters keeps the sex, drugs, and jokes zinging faster than the five ball bonus on the best pinball game ever.*

## Hooks & Slaughterhouse
Alana I. Capria
*Illustrations by Rita Okusako*

**"Once upon a hollowed out moon, my liver withers..."**

*The Bloodless girl is haunted by confusing memories of her cannibalistic worm mother. Did the Bloodless girl bury her worm mother in salt? Where have all the worm siblings gone? And how did the Bloodless girl end up on a curving rural road that leads to nowhere and everywhere?*

*The Bloodless girl can't remember. All she knows is that dust fills her arteries and the worm mother is gone. Accompanied by a skeletal pumpkin and devil tree, the Bloodless girl journeys through the New Jersey backwoods in search of a hilltop slaughterhouse that is the key to regaining her blood and learning the truth about the worm mother's disappearance.*

## The Children of Lot
Vic Kerry

**"Ye are my children. Ye are The Children of Lot."**

*Life as a middle school principal can be humdrum, and so was the case for Suzanne Clay. Everyday it was the same thing, filling out detention slips and dealing with fist fights between boys and the cliquishness among prepubescent girls. Everything changed when she met the Children of Lot and got caught up in their strange prophecy.*

*Along with Suzanne, the special education teacher and a handful of students find themselves locked in a potentially deadly and mind-altering encounter with the Children of Lot. It is an encounter that will test everything within Suzanne just to survive and get her students out of harm's way. At every step, a new danger rears its horrible head, and she battles wits with the sly and crafty leader of the cult, who will stop at nothing to make sure God smiles on his people.*

www.ingramcontent.com/pod-product-compliance
Lightning Source LLC
Chambersburg PA
CBHW050717180626
46814CB00002B/484